CHRISTMAS ON A MISSION

Hannah R. Conway

Christmas on a Mission
by Hannah R. Conway

This is a work of fiction. Names, places, characters, and events are fictitious in every regard. Any similarities to actual events and persons, living or dead, are purely coincidental. Any trademarks, service marks, product names, or named features are assumed to be the property of their respective owners, and are used only for reference. There is no implied endorsement if any of these terms are used. Except for review purposes, the reproduction of this book in whole or part, electronically or mechanically, constitutes a copyright violation.

Copyright © 2018 Hannah R. Conway
All rights reserved.
ISBN: 9781720179061
EBOOK: B07H6VRLCC

© 2018 Cover Art by Robin Ludwig Design
Gobookcoverdesign.com
© dreamstime.com

Edited by Julie Sherwood

*This book is dedicated to the teachers
I work with and know.
Your endless dedication to students inspires me.*

ACKNOWLEDGMENTS

Each story comes with a set of wonderful people to thank--some new, some still tagging along on this crazy journey with me, and I'm oh-so-blessed by their presence.

To my husband, Stephen. Babes, I love you. We truly make the best team ever. Go Team Conway!

To my kiddos. Oh how I love you both. Thank you for your encouragement, support, and bringing me delicious snacks during deadline time.

To Hannah's Heroes! My faithful cheerleaders, prayer warriors, and friends! You lovely ladies are a force of nature, and I'm so thankful to have your support!

Sara Turnquist, my friend, writing partner, sounding board, and partner in crime. Thank you!

Jessie Kirkland, with Kirkland Media Management, the most amazing agent on the planet with endless creativity. Thank you for the part you've played in my writing journey.

To my Military Spouse friends--a huge thank you! Thank you for answering my military related questions on Facebook, for your emails of encouragement, and for sharing your hearts. I'm forever thankful for the friendships Stephen and I made while in the military and now that we are out.

To Clarksville Christian Writers, a small but mighty group of writers that know how to sharpen skills. Thank you for listening to my scenes and giving thoughtful feedback.

A big 'Thank You' to Robin Ludwig from Robin Ludwig Design. Just WOW. This cover is incredible.

To Julie, my editor. Thank you for spit-shining this story. Your eye and insights were on point.

Mom, Dad, Luke...I love you guys. Thank you.

And God, just...wow...thank you. I didn't think I was going to finish this story in time, but I kept feeling you pull me along and pouring out the words. I'm ready for the next story adventure. Let's do this!

I'm certain I might be forgetting someone, and for that I apologize. Writers are crazy...that's my excuse.

I am completely aware of how many people it takes to

bring a book to fruition, and I'm reminded what a small part I play. In the end, I couldn't do it without any of you.
 Thank you. From every part of me--thank you.

Chapter One

IT'S HARD TO drive with shoeboxes blocking the rear-view mirror. As the light ahead turned yellow, Audria Rylatt pumped her brakes on the slick road to stop just in time to catch it turning red. She swatted back at the avalanche of boxes spilling into the front seat, but to no avail. The boxes poked and prodded as she shoved and heaved against them for the duration of the red light.

A car honked from behind. Wasn't like she could see much behind her, but she could see to her right and left. Two cars, one on each side, watched her with a combination of amusement and confusion.

Audria gave a slight wave and a one-shouldered shrug, face now surely the color of her hair. The woman to the right snapped a picture and continued on her way.

Great. She'd end up on one of those memes that go viral.

Audria giggled to herself and tapped on the gas.

Her tires spun for a moment, and the person honked again.

People were so impatient.

She inched forward and turned up the heat a bit more. Her breath was still icy from her bout at the mall, but she'd made out this year for sure. More boxes than ever.

The car honked again.

"That's it." Audria puckered her lips and dug her finger into the window power down button. She stuck her head out the window just in time to see the blue lights.

Her stomach dropped.

Third time in three weeks.

Audria signaled and pulled over then reached in the glove box for the necessary documents.

Please don't be the same officer. Please. Please.

Audria squeezed her eyes shut, repeating the prayer, and felt around the front seat for her purse.

"ID and insurance."

"Here, sir." Same man. Her stomach sank lower. Couldn't even look him in the eyes.

"You, again." He frowned, and instantly she focused on the mileage on her car. One hundred and twenty thousand miles on her little Accord. Due for a tune up here soon.

"Do you know why I pulled you over?"

And there she was, feeling very much like an elementary school student. "I...I wasn't speeding this time."

"Nope. I'm sure that will be next week." He chuckled at his joke, and she raised a brow. "You were swerving." He lowered his head eyeing the boxes, and Audria pinched her lip between her thumb and index finger praying her antiperspirant wouldn't fail.

"Do you know how long I've been following you?"

She winced. That seemed a sufficient answer, because honestly, she had no clue.

"I've been following you since you pulled off Madison Street."

"That long? Wow."

"You didn't see the blue lights?"

She tilted her head, and the boxes stared back. So the boxes may have been obstructing her vision. In her defense, blue lights and street lights look similar when reflecting off snow and ice. Throw in the night sky, and well--

"Ma'am?"

"No, sir. I did not see the lights."

He stared at her, thinking of what, she did not know, only that she was glad he kept it to himself.

"I'm gonna need you to step out of the car, ma'am."

"Oh, sir, I don't drink."

"Please, step out of your vehicle."

"But I have these boxes, and I'm supposed to be making cookies with my mom tonight."

"Ma'am."

She frowned, sighed, and then got out of the car careful not to slip. The officer already thought she was a drunkard.

He peeped into the car window and chuckled.

"What's so funny?"

"My wife better be drunk if she ever came home with that many shoes."

Audria folded her arms. "They're empty boxes."

"And you don't drink?"

"They're for work."

"You in the recycling business?"

She shook her head and warded off the cold by tugging her jacket close.

"Let me get this straight. You're out here on Black Friday shopping for empty shoeboxes?" He laughed, jotted something down, and wheezed. "Wait 'til the boys hear this one. Here, breathe into this."

How embarrassing.

A few cars drove past, slowing down.

Audria did as she was told. The device beeped, and he gave it a shake and a 'hmph'.

"Guess you're not drunk."

She nodded her head. "May I go now?"

He laughed and opened the door for her. "Drive careful."

Audria double wrapped the scarf around her neck before taking a seat behind her wheel. "See you soon, sir."

"You plan on getting pulled over again?"

"No." Her face warmed, and she started the car. "Good evening, sir."

He smacked his knee, nearly doubled over with laughter. Well, at least she made his evening.

***

"He didn't give me a ticket this time." Audria pinched a corner from the batch of cookie dough then rolled it between her fingers into a perfect ball and plopped it into her mouth. The sugary grains melted on her tongue. Delicious.

Perry the aging Pug waddled at her feet and grunted. That dog was the king of begging. Despite his best effort, watering eyes, and a lifted paw, Audria resisted. "It's not good for you."

"Perry, go." Mom pointed, and Perry sulked away. He gave one desperate sidelong glance over his pudgy shoulder. "Go."

Perry grumbled, and Audria swore he rolled his eyes.

"That dog." Mom sighed, both hands on her hips. "He and your father belong together."

"True." Audria nodded. If dogs and owners resembled one another, then Dad and Perry were twins--

right down to their rolly belly and grumpy personality--yet loyal and secretly soft-hearted. Audria chuckled to herself and reached for another bite.

Mom swatted at her hand. "You'll get that salmonella poisoning."

"It's worth the risk." She poked past Mom and stole another pinch.

"So, what were we talking about? Oh." Mom smiled. "I think that officer is sweet on you."

"Mom." Audria rolled her eyes and plopped on a stool sitting by the kitchen island. "He's married. And he's like sixty."

"Oh. Forget what I said then, but it wouldn't hurt to--"

"Mom, please." It's not the time. Nor will it ever be. She could never replace Clay.

"I'm just saying."

"And I'm just saying tonight was so embarrassing." Audria covered her face, reliving the entire scenario. "You should've seen him laughing at me. Someone even took a picture."

"Because you're lovely."

"Because my car was stuffed full of empty shoeboxes and a policeman was flagging me down."

"The school system is lucky to have someone who cares so much."

Audria rested her chin between her palms and wiped whatever makeup remained from her face.

"How many shoeboxes do you still need?"

"About fifty."

"Not bad at all." Mom scraped the last of the dough from the bowl and slid the dirty dish into the sink. "I bet the ladies in my Bunco group can come through for you. I'll shoot them a text."

"Thanks, Mom."

"What about supplies?" Mom clicked away on her phone to the Bunco crew. "Do you have all the items to fill them with?"

Audria ticked through the list in her mind. Soap. Washrag. Deodorant. Hairbrush. Pencils. Crayons. Toothpaste. Toothbrush. Socks. Non-perishable food items. She sighed. Homeless students needed so much more than what would fit in a shoebox.

"I'll just ask for them to send over a few things." A few more rapid thumb twitches and Mom set the phone down. "You have that look on your face again."

Audria straightened. "What look?"

"Like you believe you're not making a difference."

"We have over four hundred students this year that are considered homeless--"

"And as the school system's Homeless Liaison, you're working miracles."

"It's just a shoebox."

"We both know it's more."

Mom was right, but ... "I wish there was more I could do. Like bring them all home with me."

"In your apartment?" Mom chuckled and Audria smiled along.

She rapped her nails on the granite counter and nibbled at her thumbnail on the other hand. "You heard from Maddox?"

Mom's expression saddened. Though Mom had been a military wife, standing by Dad's side through multiple deployments, having a son deploy about drained her. "Dad talked to him yesterday."

"And?"

"He won't be home for Christmas."

Figured. "Guess it's us again."

"And it will be just as special."

And lonely. And avoiding the awkward obvious

concern on everyone's face as they watched her like some kind of cracked porcelain doll about to shatter.

Yet, their concern didn't negate the truth that people die in war. People even die on Christmas day. People like Clay.

A solid lump rose in her throat, and she forced it down to the pit of her stomach where it belonged. "Can I stay with you guys tonight?"

"Anytime." Mom leaned over and gave her a quick peck on the cheek as if she could read Audria's thoughts. "You thought about what Christmas gifts you're making this year?"

Audria was thankful for the change in conversation and nodded.

Oh, she'd thought about the gifts. Finding the time to make them was something else.

Her family had several traditions, one being all Christmas gifts were to be made or created, never bought. It stemmed from their childhood when times were tight, but had continued on and truly became a treasured tradition. Gifts ranged from baked treats, woodwork, to original songs or plays, a comedy act or two, and a whole host of other things.

"I'm thinking I might try my carpenter skills out to make your father's gift this year."

Mom's phone chimed. Two more chirps followed suit.

"Good news," Mom said. "Got more boxes and supplies. The Bunco Babes save the day."

"Bunco Babes?" Audria giggled but did a quick happy dance in the kitchen alongside Mom. A twirl, a twist, and bump the hips followed by a hug.

A clatter sounded from the upstairs landing.

"You okay, Jason?" Mom asked, wiping her hands on her Christmas-themed apron.

"I'm good, Georgie," Dad called from over the banister. "But the tree's about had it."

Audria scooted from the stool and made her way into the living room. Dad stood dangling bent pieces of faux evergreen over the railing. "Guess it's time for new one."

"The thing's as old as I am, Dad." Audria raised a brow. "Can we get a real one this year?"

Mom's smile widened as she stepped from the kitchen. "They smell so good."

"They make a mess." Dad shook a loose branch in his hand. "And It hurts when you step on the needles."

"Can you think of a better reason than that?" Mom folded her arms, head lifted toward him.

He shrugged. "Perry might pee on it."

Perry's head perked up from his bed.

"Really, Jason?"

Audria pursed her lips before she smiled. If only Maddox were here to watch this little exchange.

Dad tapped his foot and stared. He and mom were at a stalemate. Finally, he threw up his hands. "They're a fire hazard. And we've worked too hard to lose our home."

"Well then--" Mom stepped forward, both eyebrows now lifted. "Maybe Perry's pee will put it out."

Audria couldn't help but laugh. "Sorry, Dad."

"Jason." Mom's curly hair shook. "You know how much the kids loved having a real tree."

"Our kids are grown. In careers of their own."

"Really, guys, it's okay." Audria held out her opened palms.

Dad continued. "The eagles have left their nest, and an empty nest doesn't have room for a real Christmas tree."

"I'll let you think about the idiocy of that statement while your eagle, Audria, and I go pick out a tree." Mom untied her apron and tossed it over the couch. She slugged on her winter boots and reached for a coat. "Coming?"

Audria startled and grabbed her purse, still amused by the conversation. "What about the cookies?"

"They're cooling on the rack." Mom triple wrapped a knit scarf around her neck. "You coming, Jason?"

Dad grumbled like a toddler, his mustache moving mechanically over his lip. Audria sucked in her lips to keep from laughing. "It's Black Friday. People are crazy."

Perry grumbled as if in agreement with Dad.

"More reason to come protect us." Mom snatched the car keys, ignoring Dad's tantrum.

"The tree place is probably closed this time of night." He sounded hopeful.

"Extended holiday hours, dear."

"Well, I'm not staying out long." Dad stomped down the stairs. He rustled the top of Audria's hair, and she buckled under Dad's version of a love tap. "When can we have our garage back, Tooter?"

Audria cringed at the sound of the nickname but leaned in for a side hug. Dad wrapped his arm around her and squeezed until her back cracked. "I think I'll be able to get all the boxes out next week. Can I borrow the RV?"

He grinned.

"Don't laugh. It's the only thing big enough to haul four hundred shoeboxes."

"Tooter, you amaze me." He gave her another squeeze, waved bye to Perry, and they headed out the door into the frigid night air.

***

Plastic tubs and bubble wrap littered the living room floor. A plate of half-eaten cookies and pumpkin-pie crust sat on the end table beside empty hot-chocolate mugs. Audria sank into the leather couch, stomach full, and unwrapped their family's prized ornaments, placing them on top the coffee table with care. Years of collecting ornaments. These were their family heirlooms. Each ornament represented an event from the year past. Like the small, white tube-like structure she held in her palm--a rolled diploma. The year she'd graduated college--the same year Maddox was promoted to Captain in the Army and introduced her to Clay. Close to six years ago, but it seemed like yesterday. Maddox was now a Major. Clay would have been surely been a Major, too.

Audria turned the ornament over in her hand taking time to remember, but the memories began to blur. She glanced at her hand where Clay's wedding band should be, but wasn't, and could never be. Audria held her breath and placed the ornament back into the bin then reached for another ornament, something that wouldn't cause her heart to throb.

Why did Christmas have to hurt?

Momma hummed along to *Silent Night* playing on an online radio station. She squatted beneath the limbs of the evergreen and tucked a quilted tree skirt around the base of the tree. "Almost ready for the ornaments."

Dad poked at the fire and eyed the tree with a high level of disdain. Perry even eyed the tree with disgust, or maybe he plotted to pee on the trunk. Audria smiled.

"Relax, Jason." Momma paused from her task long enough to throw an arched eyebrow his way. "The flames aren't going to jump four feet from the fireplace and onto the tree."

Audria giggled, thankful for the reprieve.

"You laugh now, Tooter." Dad shook the poker stick. "There are whole TV shows dedicated to strange happenings."

Momma lifted her head. "Fireplaces gone wild are on the top of that list, I'm sure."

"You two need your own reality show."

"I like it." Dad nodded and cupped his chin. "The Grumpy Veteran and His Wife."

"Good one." Momma winked.

Audria scooped the next bubble-wrapped ornament from the container and worked to pry apart the taped edges. She smiled at her parents' banter-- family photos in front of the tree was their current topic. The tape on this little bundle didn't want to budge. Audria picked at it with her nails, but the taped split into a small sliver. First world problems were so annoying.

Mom rambled on. "My friends at Bunco taught me how to take the best pictures of Christmas lights--"

"I don't care. I'm not okay with doing a typical family photo in front of the Christmas tree," Dad said. "I see the same 'ole things all over MyFace--"

"It's called Facebook, Jason."

"Whatever it's called." He swatted at the air. "It's all a bunch of hooey."

Mom kept at her work beneath the tree, bottom in the air. Comedic really. "Then where do you suggest, Jason?"

Silence.

"Exactly. The tree it is." Mom had won. For now. Something told Audria their family Christmas photo wouldn't be in front of that tree.

Dad huffed. "Can we at least wait to take the dumb photo when Maddox comes home?"

"He's coming home?" Audria sat forward. "I thought--"

"New Year's," Dad said.

"Oh." Her heart sank, but the more she thought about it, the better it sounded. She'd take anytime she could get with her brother. "For how long?"

Dad began to help unwrap the ornaments from the

smaller bin. "Two weeks."

Not thirty days. Boo. But still. Two weeks was better than nothing.

"And--" Mom stood from beneath the tree and wiped her hands together. "That means, he'll be joining us at the cabin."

The cabin. Audria forced a grin. Every year she and her family stayed in their cabin in Gatlinburg, Tennessee to bring in the New Year. High up in the Smokey Mountains, it provided the best place to relax and catch up on life, but the cabin, so full of wonderful memories, also stood as a monument to her pain.

It's where Clay had proposed.

It's where she was when the news came. When Clay had been killed in Afghanistan on Christmas Day. Almost two years ago.

She'd been able to avoid going last year, but it seemed there'd be no missing out on returning this year.

Chapter Two

Mom and Dad had long since gone to bed, and Audria lay on the leather couch covered in an afghan her grandmother had made years ago. She rolled an edge of the yarned material between her fingers and watched the fire. It cracked and danced, the golden flames creating a warm, calming ambiance. In the corner, twinkling lights woven around the branches of the Christmas tree acted as tiny spotlights for the ornaments on display. She'd have to turn the lights off soon to keep Dad's mind at ease.

An occasional burst of wind created a hollow sound as it passed over the chimney top, but other than the sounds of a winter night, all was silent. Except her thoughts.

How could she bring herself to go back to the cabin? Didn't they know how painful it was for her to return?

Of course, they did.

They'd all--Maddox included--worked to help her move on since Clay had passed. But moving on wasn't the answer. Staying still, remembering, reliving was how she kept him alive.

But how healthy was that?

The struggle to stay in the past had somewhat pressed pause on her life. But only somewhat.

She had friends. She had fun. Laughter.

Yet, maybe Mom had a point earlier. Maybe it was time for her to date again.

Her friends would agree. Audria rolled her eyes recalling their need to set her up with practically any man that was breathing. Their intentions were kind, even if misplaced.

Audria wet her lips and buried her face in the oversized couch pillow. To love again. Yes, a part of her ached for the possibility, but to risk her heart? Once more? It had taken so long to put the pieces back together, and she still wasn't sure if her heart was whole, or if it ever would be.

She wanted Clay, but no amount of wishing would bring him back.

And that's where work came in. Working with students, families, and meeting tangible needs assuaged the ache in her soul.

Audria sighed, tugged at the afghan, and turned from the fire. There were so many more homeless children in their community than last year. Granted, homeless now included children in protective care, or not living in their parents' home, but still. The drastic increase wore on her heart.

She curled, knees drawn to her chest, and counted backward as a way to coax sleep, but sleep could not be tricked this evening.

The clock chimed two a.m. Audria rolled to her back and gazed at the ceiling. *Might as well write if I can't sleep.*

She sat up and reached for her tote near the coffee table. With a grunt, Audria slid out her journal and thumbed through the pages. Years of prayers and praises all in one place. A safe spot for her thoughts, and a place to chat with God. Audria breathed in and penned the date. She jotted down a brief summary of the day's events remembering to thank God for her family, work, and asking him to look over Maddox and the students in need. A thought gave her pause. Surely it wasn't her own. She worked to ignore it, but it came again as a whisper saying, *"Help me to move on."*

Was that God? She'd experienced that heart whisper enough to know. She swallowed, and her eyes watered. But if that's what God wanted her to pray, then so be it. Audria scribbled down the quick request just as her phone rang.

The odd number displaying on the screen meant one thing. *Maddox.*

She slid the journal to her side and snatched the phone. "Hey."

"Hey, you." Maddox sounded as happy as ever. "Happy Black Friday. It's still Friday there, right?"

"So close. Saturday."

"I'll get this time difference thing down before this deployment is up." He laughed, and she couldn't help but smile. "It's what, three a.m. there?"

"Close." She crossed her legs and drew a pillow into her lap.

"I'm sorry if I woke you up. Well, not really."

"Thanks." If Maddox were home, he'd have grabbed her into one of those terrible head rubs with her head locked under his arm. She'd poke at his ribs until he relented. "I miss you."

"You too, Sis."

"They feeding you okay?"

"Canned turkey really isn't as bad as it sounds."

Audria grimaced. "You'd eat anything."

"You take what you can get here." Maddox chuckled, and the connection filled with static. "You still there?"

Audria stood, as if that would help him hear better. She paced in front of the fireplace. "Can. You. Hear. Me?"

"Speaking louder doesn't help." He chuckled.

She rolled her eyes. "You're so weird sometimes."

"I pick on the people I care about most."

"I'm honored."

"Hey, um, I was hoping you could help me out."

"Anything."

"You know those care packages you put together for me?"

Audria nodded like he could see. She made sure to send a care package every month, fully decorated and filled with all of Maddox's favorite things that were allowed to be mailed overseas. "You need another one? You ate all those sweets already?"

"I was thinking like maybe thirty more."

"Thirty?"

"For my unit. Kind of a Merry Christmas from their leader."

She stood, processing the request. Thirty boxes. How much would that cost? And on top of the shoeboxes she was already putting together for the homeless students.

"I hear you freaking out."

"No, no. I'm, um..." Freaking out.

"They don't have to be big boxes. Something small. Like shoeboxes."

Thirty more shoeboxes. And he wanted them decorated and filled with... what? Candies. Cookies. Did he realize how much time and money she spent on individualizing his care packages? Now he wanted thirty of them?

"It's been a tough deployment for the guys. They

always get a kick out of seeing what kind of box you put together."

"I don't know, Maddox."

"I'll pay for it all."

"Maddox--"

"C'mon, Sis. Please."

He was probably making that ridiculous sad puppy face. Audria huffed. "How am I going to pull this off?"

"What about having one of the schools you work with sponsor it? 'Adopt a Unit.'"

Of course, he already had a plan. She tapped at her chin. Actually, a pretty good plan. She played out the scenario. Nora, her closest friend, was also the principal at Richland Middle. She'd probably jump at that opportunity. Maybe. But she couldn't be certain on such a short notice.

"I take it you're about to say yes?"

She groaned. "Of course."

Audria palmed her face. How on earth was she going to pull this off? She'd have to swing by Richland on Monday and beg Nora.

"Great." He cheered, and she pulled the phone from her ear. "I'll shoot you their names. Send me your account info, and I'll put the money in there."

"I want extra to cover the cost of a pedicure that I'm going to need after running all over the place putting this together."

"You don't like pedicures."

"True." She arched a brow.

"I'll throw in money to cover movie and a popcorn."

"Two movies and two popcorns."

"Deal." He chuckled. "Two movies? You seeing some--"

"Don't go there." She planted a fist on her hip. "Have you been talking to Mom and Dad?"

"No. Maybe."

"I'm fine and really quite happy with my life." Which was true. "I don't need a man like everyone keeps suggesting."

"Happy isn't what I'm worried about." His tone grew serious.

Her chest tightened. "Maddox..." But she couldn't put together a coherent thought let alone a sentence.

"I want you to live your life, Sis. Not just waiting for--"

"Just because I'm not traveling all over the world doesn't mean I'm not living. I can live and make a difference in my own community." Her face warmed, and she folded her arms, breaths short. "In fact, I'm making a huge difference in many lives."

"Defensive?"

She shrugged, working her jaw side to side. "I just don't want to keep explaining to everyone why I don't want or need to date again."

"I think we're all more concerned with--"

"I'm. Fine. But I won't be if you keep pressing me." She frowned and knelt to turn off the Christmas lights.

"Okay, okay." He huffed and the line rustled. "I love you, Sis. You know that. Just looking out for you."

His care, like every one else, was well intentioned. Audria plopped on the couch. "I'm sorry I raised my voice at you."

"It's all good. Just make sure you stuff those care packages with the cookies I like, and we'll call it even."

"Ha."

"So, the cabin, huh?"

"Wow. You go from one great topic to the next." She rested her head on the arm of the couch and pulled her hair over her shoulder.

"I'm glad we're going back."

"Yeah." Too bad the feeling wasn't mutual.

"Sis." Maddox's voice strained. "I, uh, I know this may be hard to hear coming from me, and um, it's, well, it's probably not the best time to bring this up. There's someone I want you to meet." The words sped from the receiver.

She scrunched her nose and balled her fist. "Back to that?"

"I'm serious. He's a great guy. And he'd like to get to know you."

"He's never seen me."

"I showed him your Facebook profile."

"What?" Wasn't that creeper-ish? "No. I'm not interested."

"Kind of told him you were."

"You did not." She smacked her forehead. "Undo it, Maddox."

"And he's supposed to send you a message."

"I'm not responding."

"And I kind of invited him to the cabin with us."

Her heart thudded. Tears welled in her eyes. "How could you?"

"Sis--"

"Maddox, this is too far. I'm not ready. And the cabin? Really? Why doesn't he spend time with his own family?"

"Wow, Sis."

"You know what that place reminds me of." She wiped her eyes with the sleeve of her sweatshirt. "I wish you and everyone else would stop pushing me."

"I know you're upset, but just listen."

"You listen." She gritted her teeth. "How would you like if I started trying to hook you up with my friends?"

Maddox laughed, and she huffed.

"It's not funny, Maddox."

"Nora is happily married, and the rest of your friends from work are either ancient or prudes."

She tilted her head conceding only a smidgen. "They're not all ancient."

"So, you agree the rest are prudes."

"You're impossible." Though he had a point. Most of the ladies in the office lacked a sense of humor, or even the slightest smile. "The point is--"

"Hey, Sis, I gotta go." Hurried conversation sounded in the background. "Other guys are needing to call home. Tell Mom and Dad I love them. Talk to you soon."

"Maddox," Audria growled but conceded. "I love you, too."

She held the phone in her palm until the screen went black. Thank God Maddox was at least safe, even if he was still annoying.

Thirty more boxes to fill and send.

A trip to the cabin and an unwanted guest who had a serious misunderstanding.

Merry. Christmas.

She'd rather be working.

Chapter Three

AFTER THE LONGEST Thanksgiving weekend in the history of the holiday, Audria welcomed work on Monday. Between Mom gushing over the trip to the cabin, Dad griping about the real Christmas tree and its devil needles, and Maddox's life-intruding news, the worries of work felt more like a retreat.

Too bad the school system closed for nearly three weeks over Christmas Break. Maybe there was a secret position opened that she could volunteer for. *Will work for free. Avoiding family and awkward situations like a man I don't know who thinks I'm interested.*

And how embarrassing. As if she needed help finding someone. She could if she wanted to. In a heartbeat.

She sat behind the wheel, parked in the district's parking lot, and sipped at a mug filled with warm turkey soup made from Thanksgiving leftovers--a family tradition spanning since the dawn of time.

The hodge-podge ingredients never failed to make the most delightful bowl of comfort food. After a nonstop weekend and no sign of slowing down in the weeks to come, a little comfort food was just what she needed.

She eyed the clock. The five minutes remaining of her lunch wasn't long enough to appreciate the sweet and savory concoction. Audria shrugged and tilted the mug for one last sip. The rest would have to wait until after her rounds.

The RV started up with a low rumble. A few coworkers returning from lunch break crossed the parking lot and tossed odd stares her way.

She waved, rolling down the window--not even power windows in this thing. "Have a good Thanksgiving?"

"Audria?" The older woman held a clipboard to her chest. "Did you sleep in the parking lot?"

"Huh?" The woman thought she was staying in the RV? Oh goodness. Audria turned in her seat but revved the engine on accident, startling her coworker. "Sorry. Sorry. No, um, it's shoebox season."

The two women stared, blinking.

Their smiles were crooked, like they'd never seen an RV before. Or maybe not an RV in a school district's parking lot. Audria rested her forearms on the lowered window. "You know, when we pack the boxes for our homeless students."

They nodded. "So, you're staying in an RV to..."

"Not staying." Audria laughed, but they continued to stare, both now squinting, their faces displaying obvious confusion. "Just needed a way to load up all the donations and boxes."

"Did you know it has a red nose?" said one.

"And antlers?" said the other.

"Huh?" Audria strained her neck. "Oh, yes. It's kind of my mom's idea. Make this big 'ole brown thing look like Rudolph." She giggled, but the ladies did not.

"Well...have fun," the younger one said. They whispered to one another, shoulders bumping as they hurried back to work.

Wow, Audria, you look like an idiot.

Whatever. If looking like a fool meant being able to serve each of the students in need, then so be it. She turned on the radio, then cranked it up. Though Christmas music wasn't her thing, *Jingle Bell Rock* never sounded better than when blaring from a late 1980's RV.

She made her rounds to several of the schools in the county, checking in on the students, and then stopped by the donation drop-off centers at local churches, convenience stores, and the police department to gather items for the homeless students.

A speed bump on a side road came out of nowhere, and she bounced in her seat. The seatbelt held her in place, but the cup of leftover turkey soup in the cup holder sloshed and spilled onto her knee. She dabbed it off with a wadded up napkin and worked to keep her eyes on the road.

Her phone chimed. A few cars honked as she swerved. She eyeballed the screen in quick darts.

Oh. My. Gosh.

The message.

From him. The dude who thinks she likes him.

Maddox is so going to get it.

Her face warmed, and her foot hit the wrong pedal, sending her over the next speed bump with greater speed. More soup launched into the air, and Audria hit the brake, jolting the enormous tank of an RV to a halt. Angry horns sounded. She hunched her shoulders in multiple apologies and by the grace of God, was able to pull over without causing an accident.

She took in deep breaths, inhaling and exhaling

through her nose, until her head felt light.

What is wrong with you? It's just a message.

But it wasn't just a message. It was the virtual rendition of a forced blind date. Some online, overseas version of matchmaking. An injustice. A violation of her natural rights.

She rested her forehead to the steering wheel, eyes squeezed. The phone dinged again.

One peek. That's all.

She opened one eye at a time. Facebook Messenger proudly displayed his name: Quinton Nolan.

"Dear Ms. Rylatt, I hope this message finds you doing well. I'm writing because..." but that's all Facebook would allow her to see without actually opening the message. Her finger hovered over the message bubble. One slide and she could see the rest. But then he'd know she'd seen it. Ugh. If there were some way to read it without him knowing--Facebook needed to get on that.

Seriously, Audria?

"How old am I?" She swallowed, closed her eyes. "I'm a mature, grown woman. A professional. It's only a message."

She read the short teaser again. "Dear Ms. Rylatt." So proper. What kind of man starts a message off like that?

A respectful man. The thought came from nowhere, but was nonetheless true. And a respectful man at least deserved to have his respectful message read. *I mean, he is deployed.* The least she could do was read what he had to say.

She slid the message bubble half way across the screen, heart pounding, but stopped. No. It wasn't time to read some flirty message. She had a job to do.

Audria flicked on her turn signal and waited for an opening to ease back on the road. Richland Middle's Junior Service Club was helping her fill shoeboxes today.

All four-hundred boxes. That would keep her busy enough to never even consider checking that dumb message.

***

Richland Middle School-- so it said, painted in a large red font across the back wall in the cafeteria. Home of the Raideers. A play on the word raiders, no doubt. Town legend says with an influx of white-tailed deer in the area, some local around fifty years ago thought a deer dressed in some ninja looking Viking garb paid homage to the local wildlife and the middle school's desire to...raid? Who knew for sure.

Randall the Raideer they named the him, and though no one denied the level of corniness, Randall had become quite the icon. Especially around Christmastime when Randall morphed into Randall the Rudolph Red-nosed Raideer Reindeer. A mouthful to say, but the students shouted it, chanted it, wore T-shirts declaring it, and wanted the honor of dressing like this creature at all school functions. Baffling, yet highly hilarious.

Audria shrugged at the thoughts and continued shuffling the shoeboxes down the student-based assembly line and listened as two eighth-graders argued over who would be Randall in the town's Christmas parade. She laughed to herself, thoughts drifting farther from Randall the Raideer, and shoebox packing, and more toward the message. That dumb message.

"Ms. Rylatt?"

"Huh? Yes?" Audria snapped her head to respond to the voice. The students stared at her.

"You're mixing the bars of soap in with the bags of candy again."

She mumbled a "sorry," chided herself, and emptied the box to start over. Her phone peeked from the side pocket of her purse sitting on the table. Strange how the thought of reading a simple message caused her palms to sweat.

"Got a little something on your shirt."

"Oh." Audria swiped at her blouse. Turkey soup. "Thanks, Nora."

Richland Middle was also home of Nora Wiley, the best principal in Clarksville, Tennessee, and she just so happened to be Audria's best friend since forever.

"Hey, you got your hair done."

"Girl--" Nora batted those lashes. "It's a weave."

"Couldn't tell."

"That's the point, and you're lucky I told you." She smiled and tilted her head. "Do we have enough boxes?"

"Mom's Bunco group is bringing over fifty more."

"I was being sarcastic, but wow, I can't believe we even need this many. So sad."

They both nodded.

"But I'm glad we've got you to help." Nora gave her a big squeeze. "Still on for girl's night? I've got a sitter lined up since it's Marcus's late night."

"Wouldn't miss it." Monday Trivia Night at Dos Amigos Authentic Mexican Dining was their thing. Her stomach grumbled as an after-Thanksgiving warning. Still stuffed. "I may just do chips and salsa tonight."

"I hear ya." Nora patted at her stomach. She twirled her beaded necklace around her well-manicured fingers. If only Audria could keep nails like that. The upkeep just wasn't worth it though. "Hey, I know your case load is heavy right now, but there's a student I'd like to talk to you about."

Audria dropped the shoebox, spilling the contents onto the school cafeteria floor.

"Distracted?"

"A student you'd like to talk about?" Audria squatted, and Nora followed, both scooping up the contents. "Sure thing. We can chat tonight."

"This is like the fourth box you've had to re-do. You okay?"

"Maddox--"

"He's okay?"

"Yeah, yeah. He seems to be doing well. Has a lot of free time right now." Apparently too much free time.

"Thank the Lord." Nora splayed her fingers and held them across her chest. She shifted her weight from one red high heel to the other.

A few students shuffled past carrying completed boxes in their arms, careful to stack them on the far table. Several others remained in the assembly line, each tasked with filling the box with a specific item. For five years, Richland Middle School had taken on this task. Their experience showed, and it worked like a well-oiled machine.

Audria swiped her hands and stood. "They do such a great job. Nora, I don't know how to thank you."

"These kids love helping." Nora was right. "It takes the focus off them for a while. We all need that."

So true.

Audria watched the middle school students hurry and laughed. "They're kind of like busy elves."

"Just don't call them that." Nora nudged her shoulder. "You gonna tell me what's up?"

"Maddox wants thirty Christmas-themed care packages for his unit. And I was kind of hoping you'd be interested in taking on that task."

"Of course. This group of kiddos would be honored to support our troops in that way. We'll assign students names of soldiers, we'll pack the boxes Wednesday, and ship them ASAP."

That was easy.

"And where are we going to get extra boxes?"

"Have you seen my closet?"

True. Audria nodded. Nora's shoe collection was extensive.

"But that's not the only thing on your mind."

Audria rolled her eyes. "Maddox told one of his soldiers that I was interested in him, in well, you know, *that* way."

"What?" Her face showed a mix of excitement and mortification.

"So, then the guy sends me a message on Facebook."

"What?" Her tone caused students to stare. Nora straightened her posture and tugged at her blazer, perhaps to appear more like a principal. Her nod dismissed their arched brows and tilted heads. "What did it say?"

"We sound like children."

"Whatever. What did it say?"

"I didn't read it." Audria tucked her chin and glanced at Nora from the corner of her eye.

"Girl." Nora spun on her heels. "Where is your phone?"

"Don't you dare." Audria hissed through a pasted smile, working not to draw attention.

Nora yanked the phone from Audria's purse.

"Give. Me. That."

"You have to read it first." Nora held the phone behind her back.

"I'm not ready. It's not time." Audria kept her tone low and took a step toward Nora. "You're not acting very much like a principal."

"Fine. I'll read it for you." Nora held the phone near her chest, finger pointed in swipe mode.

Audria lunged and wrist wrestled Nora and tugged. Goodness, Nora was strong. "Don't you dare read it."

"It's time, and you know it."

A large shadow hovered near. Audria stilled and released her hold on Nora's wrist. Students and volunteer staff had circled around, mouths open.

Nora cleared her throat, straightening her hair. "It's important to keep self-dense tactics sharp."

"Is that our next community service task? Self Defense lessons?" one student asked, appearing near hopeful.

"Possibly," Nora said, and Audria had to hide her face to keep the laughter building inside at bay.

"Back to work." Nora clapped her hands and then darted eyes in Audria's direction.

Audria picked up her phone and brushed her hair back.

Nora smiled and told her, "Check your phone. The message is opened." She winked and walked away leaving Audria without a single retort, only a huff.

Audria drew in the slightest breath and forced her eyes open. There it was, the message.

Here went nothing. Or something.

Dear Ms. Rylatt,

I hope this message finds you doing well. I'm writing because your brother suggested that you and I shared a mutual interest in getting to know each other. I do, however, understand that your brother likes to...embellish from time to time, and I apologize if in fact you are not interested in me. I will wait for your reply to confirm or deny your interest.

Sincerely,
Quinton

Chapter Four

Two baskets of chips and dip later, Audria contemplated unbuttoning her jeans. She swirled a piece of tortilla chip in the salsa and then in the *queso* for the perfect blend. Perfection, unlike their trivia score.

"Why are these questions so hard tonight?" Audria tapped her pencil on the edge of the table. "We're losing."

"Nothing new." Nora snorted and drew swirling designs on her trivia paper.

They both nodded in agreement and waited for the next trivia question.

"Nora, I can't thank you enough for helping with all those boxes. You're sure it's okay to keep them at your school?"

"No worries at all. It's good for our students to take part in helping their community."

"Dad's been asking for his garage back. Wonder when he'll ask for the RV back?"

Nora laughed, palming her soda. "I don't think anyone would ask for that thing back."

"What? You won't help me deliver boxes in the 'Reindeer?' It's practically the definition of school spirit." Audria used her best sly grin.

"I'll tell you the definition of school spirit." Nora shook a chip in one hand and the trivia notepad with the other. "Wearing that two-hundred-degree costume with a red blinking nose, while bouncing on a trampoline and trying to make half court shots during the Thanksgiving student assembly."

Audria couldn't hold in her laughter. "You win. You've definitely got school spirit. I hereby free you from passing out boxes with me in the RV."

"Girl, you know I got your back."

"You could wear the Randall costume while I drive!"

"Don't push it."

"Last question," the DJ called from his corner stand.

She and Nora moved to the edge of their seats.

"Who was... the... first woman... to be... inducted into the Rock 'n Roll Hall of Fame?" asked the DJ.

Audria scratched her head. They were so losing tonight.

"I've got this." Nora stood waving her paper in hand. "Aretha Franklin," she whispered to Audria.

Audria formed an O with her mouth. She high-fived Nora, and they took their ten points like it might have been a hundred.

Nora shrugged. "At least we got some points."

"We've won before."

"Like once." Nora laughed. "A year ago."

"I mean, c'mon. What normal person knows the scientific name for a dolphin?"

"They did." Nora pointed with the tip of a chip in the direction of the center table.

"They don't count. They're doctors or something."

"Well, they didn't know about Ms. Aretha Franklin,

did they?"

True. Audria laughed.

"Maybe trivia isn't what's on your mind tonight."

Heat rushed to her face. Audria coughed and covered her mouth. "You wanted to talk to me about a student, right?"

"So, you're gonna write him back, right?" Nora sipped on her soda.

"Let's chat 'student' first, and then the other 'thing' later."

Nora frowned but nodded. "It is important."

"What's up?"

Nora looked from side to side. Audria was sure she was making certain no familiar faces filled the restaurant. "He's not homeless, or we don't think he is, but his teachers have flagged him as a concern. Hygiene, poor performance, so hungry." She folded and unfolded her hands on the table, eyes watering. Audria offered a gentle smile. Richland Middle was lucky to have such a caring principal looking out for their students.

Audria pressed her back against the cushioned booth. "Have you reached out to the family?"

"Yes, but no contact has been made yet." Nora frowned.

"Does he appear abused in anyway?" A tough question to ask, but an essential one at that. She'd seen too many children hurt and made it a point to step in when the situation needed.

Nora shook her head. "Just something about him has us all concerned. That gut feeling, you know?"

Audria nodded. "Does his attendance warrant a welfare check?"

Nora scrunched her nose and squinted. "Would you mind?"

"It's part of my job." The part she took most serious.

"We've called and called. He's missed so many days." Nora snapped a chip into small pieces, eyes drawn tight. "This kid has so much potential, and we are concerned. Same clothes. Distant and withdrawn. Like he's on the cusp of one way or the other, you know?"

Oh, she knew. Audria had been around long enough to see what poverty did to students. When basic needs were not met... well, thinking about a future was near impossible. It broke her heart. She worked hard to see to it every child in their district had their needs met.

"Shoot me a name and an address, and I'm on it first thing in the morning."

"Okay, no more sad tonight. Happiness only. Back to 'the message!'" Nora's tone exaggerated, her hands outstretched wide. "So, what did you think about it? I mean, that message, was so, so..."

"Mannerly. Respectful. Robotic. From the nineteenth century."

"And more," Nora said through a sappy sigh and a smile. "Very transparent and forthcoming."

"Totally intimidating."

"No way. Just a guy who's honest. Those are hard to find, my friend." She pointed a finger. "I thought I'd snagged the last one." Nora winked and reached for another chip.

The mariachi band carousoled around a nearby table playing festive Christmas tunes. "Away in a Manger" sounded funny on an accordion.

Audria rested her forearms on the lacquered surface of the table and took in the atmosphere. The place was full of smiling faces, relaxed expressions, families and friends engrossed in conversation. Truly lacking nothing, like her, happy and full--at the moment-- literally full. Her eyes bulged at the site of a fresh basket of chips the waiter placed between her and Nora.

"I don't see the point of responding." Audria rapped her fingers. "I'm not some desperate person vying for the affection of a man."

"Which makes it a pretty good time to date. Desperate people make desperate decisions. You..." Nora squinted, head tilted. "You're distracted. On purpose. Because staying busy and helping others means you don't have to think about yourself."

Audria wiggled in her seat, Nora's words holding her hostage.

Nora leaned over the basket of chips. "Distracted people can make dumb decisions, like not responding to a Facebook message from a man with courage enough to express interest."

The waiter approached, steaming plates high above his head, and then placed the plates on the table. Grilled peppers, onions, and chicken smothered in white *queso* served over a bed of rice. By now, both her stomach and head were full.

"Why did I order food?" Audria grimaced eyeing her plate.

"Just unbutton the top button on your pants. Works every time."

Audria grinned and shook her head. "Maybe I am distracted... or busy on purpose."

Nora bobbed her head in between bites. "Now we're making progress. Write him back."

Audria blew out her cheeks and reached for her phone. "I don't know."

"You kind of have to."

Audria raised a brow, and Nora shrank back into the booth, a slick grin on her face. "What do you mean?"

"I messaged Maddox."

"And?"

"Let him know I'm happy to help with the boxes for

his unit."

"So?"

"So, he sent me a list of the names.."

"Still not tracking."

"I've already assigned soldiers to students, and it appears that--"

"No." She and Maddox wouldn't dare do it.

Nora grinned and pulled a slip of paper from her purse. "One soldier remained."

Audria shook her head. "You didn't"

"I did." Nora plucked a slip of paper from her purse and slid it across the table. "Congratulations. It appears you're in charge of putting together Quinton's Christmas box."

Audria sat glaring at her friend, temperature rising.

"So, it's a good thing you're writing him back."

Audria smacked her hand over the name and wished more than anything her eyes had the capacity to shoot laser beams, or slime, or something gross and awful.

"Don't look at me like that." Nora frowned, her entire body in a pout. "No harm in helping. Besides, it's close to Christmas. You'd really say no to sending a deployed soldier some source of holiday happiness?"

When she put it that way. Audria groaned. "I'm not the bad guy here."

"No one is. It's a win-win."

Sure. A win-win. *We'll see.*

Audria reached for her phone, and Nora all but hovered over the screen.

"Do you mind?" Audria shielded the screen with her shoulder, and Nora slunk back into her seat.

A quick message. Short and sweet.

Audria drew in a deep breath, held it, and wrote back.

***

Her thumbs tapped out a quick message, deleted it three times, and after Nora's aggravated huff, she settled on a simple, "Hello."

"Go on, go on." Nora waved her hand, and Audria sneered.

"Don't rush me." Audria crossed her ankles and eyed the screen. To press send or not to press send--that was the question.

Nora strained her neck. "That's all you're writing? A 'hello'?"

"What? It's nice."

Nora palmed her forehead. "Please say something more. Anything. Like 'yes, my brother was right, I'm interested.'"

"But I don't know if I'm--"

"Just add more."

"Hello, Quinton. Thank you for getting in touch. You're right--" Audria tilted her head, thumbs clicking the screen. "My brother does embellish."

Audria paused. "How does that sound?"

"Like you aren't interested. Try again."

"Fine." Audria groaned and shoveled a mix of the veggies into her mouth and chewed, praying more words would come. She played the sentence over in her mind and continued. "I am willing to get to know you. Where should we start?"

And send. Audria hit the button and slid her phone from view, much more interested in her food, though the knots forming in her stomach beat down her appetite.

"I'm proud of you." Nora nudged her with a quick kick under the table. "Wanna know what he looks like?"

Audria's jaw dropped. "You're stalking him?"

"What? I've got to know what kind of man is trying to get with my bestie."

"Get with? That sounds trashy. I don't 'get' with

people."

"Date. Hang out. Talk. Go steady." She rolled her eyes and scrolled through her phone. "Get your mind out of the gutter." Nora stuck the phone in Audria's face. "Here. Look."

Whoa. Audria swallowed. Was she blushing? "He's..."

"Fine."

Audria nodded, no denying that much. Those eyes. That creamy colored skin. "He's black?"

"Mixed actually."

How in the world did Nora know this? Silly question. Nora knows all.

"I didn't expect that." Clay had been two shades whiter than herself. They'd often laugh about having to buy stock in sunscreen for their children one day. Audria turned from the photo. Maybe she really wasn't ready to move on.

"Girl. His name is Quinton. How many white guys do you know with that name?"

"I dunno. Guess I never thought much about it." She shrugged and slumped, eyeing the paleness of her skin. "His skin is so nice, and I have...freckles."

"So?" Nora's lips twisted. "If they'd all go together, you'd be tan."

Audria laughed and conceded.

"Well, I've got it all planned out. The two of you get married, and your kids will have the cutest hair. I can teach you how to do little black girl hair, well, mixed girl hair, which is similar."

And Nora would. She gave Audria the 411 on hair. The woman even made a lot of her own hair products.

"Hold on." Audria held up a palm. "No one is getting married yet, and we sure aren't talking about having kids." She had enough students to think about without adding any of her own yet.

Nora waved a hand. "How long do you think it will take to hear back from him?"

Audria shrugged and shuffled the food around on the steaming skillet. Her phone buzzed and her heart stopped. She and Nora glanced at the phone and then stared at each other.

"No way." A smile grew on her friend's face.

Audria picked up the phone. The message read, "May I call you?"

She didn't have to read it to Nora. Her crazed bestie pushed herself across the table. "Yes. Yes, he can call you. Check, please." She called to the waiter.

"We just got our food."

"Who can eat now?"

Good point. "Wait. How did he get my number?"

Nora rolled her eyes. "Who else?"

"Maddox." Audria gritted her teeth.

The mariachi band waltzed by playing a strange version of "Rudolph, the Red-Nosed Reindeer". Nora all but dragged Audria from the booth. Audria stumbled and dug into her purse and tossed two twenties on the table.

"That'll cover it," she said and waved to the waiter who bore the most perplexed look on his face. "Um, Feliz Navidad?" She offered him the extent of her Spanish and holiday spirit before Nora huffed.

"We've got things to do," she said, and out the door they went.

Audria's head spun. Her pulse thumped to a rhythm all its own. Why had she ever responded to that message, and why in the world was she even contemplating starting a conversation with a complete stranger? Audria paused, but Nora tugged. And if Nora thought she was listening in on this phone call, well...maybe she'd have to listen from a distance.

Chapter Five

QUINTON SAT ON the edge of his cot, back hunched, and elbows digging into the tops of his knees. He should be asleep right now. All the other soldiers were. Something about racing thoughts, and the heat, or maybe remaining adrenaline from their last mission hadn't left his system yet. Either way, sleep evaded him.

He cradled his cell in one hand and tapped each number carefully. The glow of the screen lit up his room like daylight, and Quinton was thankful for the lack of a roomie. Rank has its privileges. Drawbacks, sure, but not sharing a room-- definitely a privilege.

Beads of sweat dampened the creases of his forehead, and Quinton worked both knees in a pump. Years of not dating, and now he decides to connect, while deployed? He shook his head. What in the world was he thinking?

Major Rylatt was a trustworthy guy and all that, but the thought of getting involved with his superior's sister made Quinton's stomach pinch and twist. Joining the Army had helped him stay out of trouble, not get in it.

Quinton hovered his index finger above the last digit. His stomach was in a vice.

But it was time. Something about turning thirty made a man reevaluate his life. And now, well, surrounded by mountains and desert, he'd had time to reevaluate.

Yeah, he traveled. Saw things. Did adrenaline-junky things. But without someone to share life with...it all seemed pointless. Even Army life, as much as he loved it, seemed...off, without someone there to love and to love him back. God even said it wasn't good to for man to be alone, so He made woman--God was right, as usual. No sense in arguing with the Creator of the Universe.

But Major Rylatt's sister? And after everything she'd been through?

Quinton sucked on his bottom lip. He'd seen the packages come in like clockwork. All decorated, organized, and packed to the brim. Audria cared for her brother and the other soldiers. Major Rylatt shared the treats. The sugar cookies were great, but those macarons she made were always on point.

And the woman was a saint, working as a Homeless Liaison for the local school system. Wow. Definitely the kind of woman he'd have been proud to show off to his mom. Before she passed, she'd prayed for Quinton to find a godly woman to love him and others. A strange prayer for a twelve-year-old boy, but now, the prayer made sense.

But maybe he should wake Major Rylatt up just to make sure he had permission to get to know Audria. *No. No.* Quinton hung his head and rocked it back and forth. Major Rylatt told him to call her. Pretty much hadn't stopped harassing him about it.

"C'mon, man." Quinton huffed, giving himself a pep talk. He'd had enough nerve to seek her out; surely he had enough nerve to make the call. And what if the whole thing crashed and burned? He'd been down that road before. Quinton physically shook the thought and hit the call button. He closed his eyes, whispered a prayer, and listened to the phone ring.

One ring. Two. Then three.

"Hello?" Her voice was sweeter than expected. Younger. Too young? Naw. Three years' difference wasn't bad at this age. "Is this Quinton?" And her voice shook. Possibly from nerves? He understood.

Quinton cleared his throat. "Ms. Rylatt?"

"Please, call me Audria."

"Audria it is then." It sounded nice. "Thank you for allowing me to call."

Silence.

Was he too formal? Too proper? He'd been taught to respect everyone, especially women. "They're life givers," his mother would say, and all life is to be protected and honored. Lots of folks thought being in the Army was a strange way to protect and honor life, but it made perfect sense to him.

"Ms. Audria?"

"Please, just Audria."

"Yes, ma'am." Oh, man, did he just call her ma'am? He scratched at his temple and rubbed a thumb along the corner of his lip. His mind emptied. Um. Um. And Audria wasn't talking either. Maybe this whole thing would crash and burn before it began.

"Look, Quinton." Her voice shook and then steadied. "Really, thank you for calling, but--"

"Let's just talk." Where did those words come from? Wherever they'd come from, he was thankful.

"Okay." She paused. "I'm not sure what to talk about."

"Macarons?"

"Huh?" She giggled. That was a good sign.

"You make amazing macarons." Wow, what an idiot thing to say. But true. Of all the ways to start a conversation...geez.

"Well, um, thank you." Another giggle. "I can give you the recipe?"

A quick frustrated whisper sounded on the line. Quinton squinted as if it helped him hear better. Audria offered a muffled apology to the voice.

"Is this an okay time to talk?"

"Yes, yes, I'm sorry. It's just my friend. She seems to be way too interested in our conversation and feels macaron recipes isn't a suitable topic."

"Oh." Guess her friend had a point.

"I'm dropping her off at her house now. Bye, Nora." The low, frustrated, whispered grumble returned. "Bye. See you later. Bye for real, Nora." The grumble continued but faded. Audria must be driving away.

Quinton laughed. "Sounds like you and I both have people spying in on us."

"It's frustrating for sure."

"Annoying."

"You totally get it."

"Your brother is--"

"The definition of annoying, I know. But I love him."

"He's a great guy and thinks highly of you. Real protective."

"Which is why I guess we're having this conversation."

The silence returned. Should he break it? Quinton opened his mouth, but Audria beat him to it.

"Quinton, you seem like a great guy, but..."

Her hesitation was all he needed. "Audria, I know."

"You know?"

"That you were engaged, and how...or...what happened to Clay...and..." Quinton paused. What kind of conversation was this? From macarons to the death of her fiancé. He smacked his forehead. "I'm sorry, Audria. You know, we can--"

"It's okay. I'm okay. And I'd like very much to get to know you better."

"Really?"

"Really."

"So..."

"Want to start with my famous macaron recipe?"

"You've got my attention." Quinton scooted back on his cot, back pressed against the plywood wall in their makeshift quarters. He crossed his feet at the ankles and soaked in her voice. She talked quick, with a smile in her voice. Hint of a southern drawl, but educated. Not brash, but her own kind of bold. And the woman spoke with confidence, with intention, like making macarons could change the world. And maybe they could, or at least the woman behind the mixing bowl could change his world.

Chapter Six

THIS MUCH SHE knew-- Quinton Nolan awoke feelings she was once certain were dead. Feelings of? Audria placed a hand over heart. Feelings of hope. Like maybe, just maybe, she could love again.

No hiding a smile tonight. Her phone buzzed. Nora again.

Well, Nora would simply have to wait. Tonight was hers. Hers to process and relive.

She had talked to Quinton for three hours. Three. Hours. About what?

Audria paused and continued to comb the shelves of Walmart. No one in their right mind could sleep after spending three hours engaged in the most interesting conversation with the most interesting guy. Solution? Get started on packing Quinton's shoebox Christmas gift from Maddox. Though the store was near empty at midnight, buying items to fill one Christmas box proved challenging, especially when her mind was elsewhere.

What *had* she and Quinton talked about?

Nothing in particular, but so much.

Macarons.

Nora. Maddox. Her parents. Real Christmas trees versus the fake kind. RVs. Turkey soup. Shoeboxes. Speeding tickets.

Middle School. Randall the Rudolph Raideer--he'd laughed close to uncontrollable at that one.

But not Clay. No, she couldn't bring herself to go there, to have that conversation. His name still made her heart wince.

Audria took in a slow breath and let it go. What else had they talked about?

All the places he'd traveled.

How he read a lot, mostly non-fiction, but that was okay. Though, fiction was way better.

Audria turned the cart and made her way down another aisle.

Crunchy peanut butter was his favorite. And easy to pack. She grabbed two containers of it from the shelf and continued to fill her cart with anything edible and Christmas themed. Her mind snapped back to the conversation with Quinton.

He hailed from Atlanta, Georgia. Cheered for the Georgia Bulldogs--but that could be forgiven. Never tried shrimp--must fix that. Was into Spartan races--those crazy people who run with concrete filled buckets, throw spears, and all the other things that make her squishy pale skin tremble in fear. She could cheer him on from the sidelines.

His father was a pastor overseas, and cancer took Quinton's mother when he was in middle school. Her heart ached. A terrible loss at such a pivotal time in a child's life.

He had run away from home as a young teen. Was homeless, got into some trouble, which was a large part of the reason Quinton joined the Army at seventeen.

Christmas was his favorite holiday. Audria swallowed, hands gripping the cart handle.

He'd gone on and on about how much hope Christmas brings to the world. The birth of Jesus, the Savior of the World, a promise of peace and to right the wrong.

Audria nodded at the conversation recalled. No denying the truth in Quinton's statements, but no denying the truth in hers. Christmas hurt. And for hundreds of students in her county who were considered homeless, Christmas meant a time of desperation.

***

Tuesday morning--just over three weeks until Christmas break. Dread typically followed the thought of a long break, especially Christmas, but maybe time off wouldn't be so bad. Time off that involved meeting Quinton--no. Audria refused to let the thought go any further. She stretched back in her office swivel chair and stifled a yawn. Three and a half hours of sleep meant this would be a non-stop coffee kind of day.

Her phone chimed at her desk, and Audria swiped the screen.

You know you have to fill me in on the convo with your soldier boy.

Audria rolled her eyes but smiled. **Will do. So tired. We talked forever.**

Nora replied with a chicken happy dancing emoji.

Audria tilted her head and recalled a bit of her conversation with Quinton. **He's...different.**

???

In the best way.

Whew! You had me worried. When is he calling you again?

Dunno. *But I hope it's soon.* She twirled a piece of her hair around her finger like a middle school girl. **You**

know how the Army works.

Girl, you know I do. We're packing the boxes for the unit Wed, right?

Yeah. Got macarons ready for Quinton's box and sugar cookies for the other guys.

You made them? Last night? Girl.

I couldn't sleep.

She sent a series of floating hearts. **I hear wedding bells.**

That's just the tardy bell ringing in the hallway. Get back to work.

Bahahaha. Good one. Ok. Sending you the name of the student and address.

Thx.

Audria waited for the chime, and pushed aside the pang in her stomach when it came. No matter how long she'd been doing this job, seeing the names of children in need or in harm's way hurt.

Jayce Dickens, 13 yrs old. 2112 Southridge Place. Unit F.

An address was a good sign, but didn't necessarily mean the child had a home. Many addresses were false, or reflected students living with friends or a family member, or sometimes a complete stranger.

Thx for doing this. I know your plate is full. See u tomorrow. XOXOX -Nora

Audria replied. **Got one more call to make then on my way. :)**

A heavy sigh worked its way from her lungs. She tapped out a rhythm on her desk and rolled her chair toward her work phone, careful to unravel the cord. She punched in a number and let it ring. Connection calls were vital. Churches, local businesses, really anyone willing and able to help made all the difference to the students in need.

Today alone, two local Methodist churches agreed to donate their parking lot over the long break for families living out of their cars. One Presbyterian church agreed to convert their gym to a clothing store for students and families in need. And a Baptist and a Catholic church joined forces to open their doors during the winter months to families living on the streets. If this connection call was a success, then a third church would be added to the mix. The least she could do was work to secure safe locations for the students over the long break, and prayerfully even longer.

The phone rang. Rang some more. No answering machine picked up. She'd simply have to stop by in person. That often did the trick.

Audria scanned her notepad and daily agenda. Filled, but nearly done--and the work day wasn't even half over. Satisfaction. Not a bad morning at all. In addition to the connections made earlier this morning, three local food pantries and one food truck had donated their services to provide hot meals over the holiday. Combined with the shoebox gifts, well, maybe the families could have a Merry Christmas. Her heart warmed.

She stood, grabbed her coffee and dragged a finger down the scribbled-out notes, stopping at the bottom of the page--dinner with Mom and Dad. She made a mental note to call Mom before heading over for the evening, typed in the directions on the GPS phone app, waved to her colleagues, and headed out.

Traffic was light, and no red lights interfered.

"You have arrived at your destination," said the automated voice.

Here. An older apartment complex just off the interstate.

"Thank you." Ugh. Audria shook her head. "I just said thank you to a computer."

She stepped from her car, coffee and phone in hand. Unit F. Hmm. Right. There.

She squinted to see past the bright white sky and shivered, warding off the cool winter air. Her wedge-heeled boots crunched in the remnants of snow. Winter had come early this year. Most of the snow and ice had finally made their retreat to the sides of the sidewalks, stacked like the walls of a fort. Forts like she and Maddox made as children for chucking tightly packed snowballs at each other. Mom and Dad had joined in on more than one occasion.

No white flags were ever raised in a Rylatt snowball feud. 'Mission first, at all cost,' Dad would yell, hurling the snow at the opposing fort. Serious business. Audria laughed and sipped her coffee.

Inevitably, she, Maddox, or even Mom would take a snowball to the face. Dad celebrated being the victor with an unabashed dance in the front yard while the victim cried, hand over the wound. He and Mom would get in a tiff, but amends were made by all over mugs of steaming homemade hot chocolate. And the next day, part two of the Rylatt Snowball Wars continued. Even into adulthood.

Would Quinton one day join in the snowy fight? Audria grinned making a mental note to ask his opinion on all things snow related.

Clay had joined the ranks for several years, giving Dad some serious competition. Audria picked up her pace and waited for the pain and grief that accompanied memories of Clay to pang her heart and mind. But they didn't come. No pain, only a sweetness. Bittersweet, yes, yet more sweet.

What did this mean?

Audria steadied her breathing as she stepped onto the small porch and gave pause before knocking. One never knew what to expect. 'Plan for the best. Expect the worst,' Dad had told her before she took this position. On more than one occasion, she wished his advice to be false.

Audria whispered a prayer and knocked.

The door opened, and a woman, perhaps her age, answered. Large, questioning eyes peered at her. "May I help you?"

"My name is Audria, and I'm with the School System--"

"I was wondering when I'd hear from you." Her voice filled with defeat.

"So, this is the home of Jayce Dickens?"

The woman nodded, and a sense of relief washed over Audria. This child had a home. Wasn't living in a tent, or in a car, or under a bridge.

"And you're his mother?"

The woman nodded once more. "We're not bad people."

"Oh, no, ma'am, I would never think that." A half lie. "But we are concerned about Jayce's attendance. Could we talk?"

The woman opened the door wider and gestured Audria inside.

A simple home. Humble. Tidy. Normal. Maybe one, no, two bedrooms. Tiny kitchen that served its purpose. A baby blanket lay on the floor with a few blocks and a stuffed animal. No Christmas tree or any Christmas decorations to be seen. Hmm. That was an easy fix.

"Please. Sit." The woman fixed at her hair and sat on the couch.

Audria sat adjacent in a rocking chair. "Is Jayce home?"

"He's sleeping right now."

It was nearly 11:30 a.m. Was he sick? The woman

offered no additional information.

"May I call you, Ms. Dickens?" She nodded, and Audria continued, "Is there a reason for Jayce's continued absences? An illness, injury?"

Ms. Dickens swallowed, head lowered. She held her hands in her lap and rocked slightly. "I try to homeschool him so he stays up on his schoolwork."

"But is there a reason? I'm here to help in any way."

"I don't know what else to do." She lifted her head, eyes watering, and clasped a hand over her mouth.

Was it drugs? Audria prayed that not be the case.

"We can't help if we don't know what's going on. We're all very worried. Please." Audria leaned forward resting an elbow on her knee.

Ms. Dickens' shoulders slumped, and her face grew a pained expression. Her young face aged before Audria's eyes. "Jayce's father left us. We weren't married."

She paused as if awaiting judgment, but Audria pressed her to continue.

Ms. Dickens sighed. "I have a GED, a criminal record--but that was from years ago," she assured. "And I'm working two jobs. I'm trying to get things in order to apply for college or a tech school, but--" She wiped at her eyes.

Audria's throat burned. Goodness these stories hurt to hear.

Ms. Dickens continued. "We don't have a car. No Internet."

And then it made sense. Ms. Dickens working two jobs and the baby blanket on the floor.

The realization nearly stole her breath. "Jayce is babysitting when you're at work."

Ms. Dickens covered her face, but it didn't hold back the tears. "Please, don't take my son. Please forgive me."

"It's okay. It's okay. We're not here to take Jayce."

Audria placed her hands on Ms. Dickens' knees. "We can help, but you have to let us."

"I don't know where to begin to ask, and I'm worried Jayce is hanging out with gang members, and--"

"What makes you think that?" Audria remembered the conversation she had with Nora. How Nora and the teachers were concerned Jayce was on the cusp of going down a bad path.

"He's such a good kid." Ms. Dickens sniffled. "And I know he worries about me and his baby brother. This isn't the best neighborhood and some of his buddies are known gang members." She sucked in a deep breath, her entire body now trembling. "And he's been coming home with cash to give me and leaving the house at odd times. Oh God. This is all my fault."

"Ms. Dickens, we're going to help you, and we're going to help Jayce." Audria reached over and grabbed Ms. Dickens into, a hug and a simple truth settled into Audria's mind. Helping students succeed often meant helping their families succeed.

Chapter Seven

A WEEK PASSED. This most recent mission took longer than they had at first thought. Thankfully no one was injured other than a few bumps and bruises, and now all the men were mere footsteps from their cots and a semi-hot shower.

The pull to get back to the FOB, Forward Operating Base, grew by the minute. Keeping Audria from filling his thoughts was a serious struggle. He'd been able to do his job and do it well, but in the quiet moments, her voice returned. Quinton smiled, walked down the hall and into his room. Home sweet home. For a bit longer at least, and then? He sighed. Go back to Fort Campbell and wait for the next assignment, the next deployment. But this time, maybe he'd have someone to come home to? The thought brought hope.

He checked his watch. She'd be sleeping right now. No need to wake her. The woman seemed to run on caffeine and sunshine; disrupting her at this hour would be an injustice to society. Instead, he lounged and rubbed a hand over his face, stifling a yawn.

Young G.I.s argued over the showers, and loud music blared from their rooms. Quinton balled a fist ready to bang on the wall, but who was he to kill their fun? All soldiers had their own way of unwinding after a mission. He wished loud music wasn't one of those ways, but whatever. He'd give them ten minutes and then a warning.

He bent, body protesting, as he leaned to untie his boots. They fell with a thud, and he rolled to his side, pulling his phone from the cinder block nightstand.

Several missed messages. From Audria. Quinton sat up, jerking his cot from the wall.

He scrolled, smiling at each message.

A Bible verse. And then another. A "Thinking of you and watching Netflix. Are you cool with chick flicks?" message. A prayer for protection. A pic of hot-chocolate macarons. Another pic of her sitting with a crew of students as they posed in front of stacked shoeboxes. He laughed out loud at the last pic. She stood bundled to the chin in a winter coat and posed with a painting of Randall the Rudolph Raideer Reindeer.

This woman. Wow. Quinton cupped his chin as he continued to scroll. What was it about Audria that made him want to never live without her?

"Hey." Major Rylatt barged in. Quinton stood and saluted.

Major Rylatt swatted at the air. "Salute me later."

"Yes, sir." Quinton nodded.

"Are those messages from Tooter?"

"Tooter?"

"Audria."

"You call her, Tooter?" *Oh, this was too good.* Quinton let a small chuckle slip.

"Dad started it." Major Rylatt set his arms akimbo. "Be sure to ask her how she got that name."

"I'm not even sure if I want to know." Quinton laughed and gestured at a rickety camping chair. "Stay awhile."

Juggling the whole 'boss, but still friends thing' proved a challenge, yet, Major Rylatt was a great guy.

Major Rylatt sat and stretched his legs. He sank back into the old chair with a grimace, scooted a bit, and then grinned. "Much better. Now, tell me how things are going."

"I mean..." Quinton's mind drew a blank. Didn't Major Rylatt know how awkward this was? "So, here's the thing...you're my boss, and..."

"I get it. I do, but you can't leave me hangin' after I got the ball rolling."

"She's..." *Amazing. Incredible. Everything I've ever wanted.*
"I knew you'd like her."

Like didn't seem to fit. His heart thumped. Could it be?

Quinton breathed a silent prayer. *Could it be, Lord? Is she who I've been waiting for?*

No possible way. He'd only been talking to her less than two weeks.

This wasn't some movie. And love at first message wasn't a thing.

"You okay, man?" Major Rylatt's laughter brought him to.

"Oh, um. Yeah. Tired. Long mission, you know?"

Major Rylatt rubbed his hands together and smacked his knees. "I've got some news sure to wake you up."

Quinton tilted his head.

"Got word we'll be leaving here on the 20th."

"Two weeks?"

Major Rylatt nodded.

"We'll be home for Christmas?"

"That's right. The Commander asked if there was

anyone willing to move their leave around, and I jumped at the opportunity." Major Rylatt stood. "Hello cabin, here we come."

The news, yes, beyond exciting, but stomach pinching, too.

"Forgot to tell you, if you're wanting to get gifts, don't bother."

"I can't just come to your family's cabin and not bring gifts."

"We make our presents."

"What?" Quinton worked to keep his jaw from unhinging.

"Yeah, it's kind of a thing we do in our family."

"So, like, arts and crafts type of stuff?"

Major Rylatt fanned his hand side to side. "Kind of. More like homemade gifts. Think 'things from the heart.'"

"I'm thinking I have no crafting or gift-making skills."

"No worries. You'll think of something."

Quinton raised both brows and held in a breath. The likelihood of coming up with a homemade gift to give Audria or anyone in the Rylatt family was slim. "What's your gift?"

"Not telling."

From this angle, Major Rylatt seemed more like a kid than his boss.

Quinton frowned. "C'mon, sir. You can't spring this kind of info on me and not help."

"Audria will love whatever you make for her."

"And the rest of the family? Sir, I can't even successfully paint a rock."

Major Rylatt burst into laughter. Glad this was funny for him. "But you can shoot a gun like it's an art form."

"I doubt your family will want shooting lessons for

Christmas."

"Now you're thinking."

"Of what?"

"Of things outside the box."

"That's loads of help." Quinton rolled his eyes. Talk about a way to end up on a family's bad side--mess up their Christmas traditions with homemade, crafty gifts gone all kinds of wrong.

"You're worried over nothing. It'll be fun."

Nothing about DIY Christmas gifts sounded fun.

Major Rylatt smacked a palm on Quinton's shoulder. "One year, I did a comedy act for the whole family. That was my gift to all of them. I've made slide shows, home movies while deployed. I've wrapped little vials filled with dirt from the different places I've traveled. Really, just something that says you took your time to think of something a little different and special."

Quinton shook his head. This would be interesting. "You tell Audria we're coming home early?"

"Nope." Major Rylatt locked his fingers behind his head and grinned. "She's fun to surprise."

His stomach fluttered--an unmanly feeling for sure, but he couldn't deny the pull to meet her.

Coming home early-- awesome. Actually meeting Audria--best news ever. Having to make Christmas gifts for everyone--ugh. Quinton groaned. Maybe he'd visit his father in India instead. Surely Pops could use the help.

"Sir--" Quinton eased to his feet. "I've never met anyone who could deliver the best news packed with the worst news."

Major Rylatt made his way to the door. "It's a gift."

Clearly.

Chapter Eight

"I KNOW I can't save the world, Mom." Audria pushed the cart down the home improvement store aisle, the scent of fresh pine and motor oil following close behind. She unbuttoned her red wool jacket, but heat continued to climb up her neck. Not anger, no. Audria chewed on her bottom lip. Okay, maybe a bit of anger.

Mom picked up her pace, curls still bobbing when she caught up. "I'm just saying, trying to help students and their families is wonderful, and you should, but--"

"But what?" Audria stopped and faced her mom. Her frustration eased upon seeing the concern in her mother's eyes.

"But I want to see you taken care of, too. Where's your happy ending?"

Audria gave a half smirk. "I don't particularly want an ending, Mom."

Mom swatted at her shoulder. "It does sound a little morbid, happy 'ending.'" Her tone dropped an octave. "It should be more like, 'happy life' or, oh, here's what I've been looking for."

The heavy moment dissipated as they paused in front of drills and saws and all things that looked like Mom might lose a finger.

Audria made a face. "A Dremel tool?"

"A Dremel 4000." Mom smoothed her hand over the display.

"What exactly are you making Dad for Christmas this year?"

Mom swung her wrist, eyebrows arched. "That's for me to know--"

"And me to find out. Yeah, I got it." No questions around this time of year. But whatever Mom was cooking up or crafting for Dad, Audria prayed it didn't end up with a hospital visit.

Audria leaned over the handle of the cart while Mom compared saws. Her thoughts drifted between Quinton, how much she wanted him to call again, and work-- rather, the young boy, Jayce, and his mother, in need of so much more than she could offer.

"Look at this." Mom gasped, and Audria snapped back to aisle eight with concrete floors and hardcore hand tools.

Mom had made her way to an end-cap filled with knit Christmas sweaters for dogs. In a home improvement store? Seriously bad product placement.

"Perry would love this."

"Would he?" 'Cause the Perry the Pug Audria knew would hate it. Might possibly eat on it. Or pee on it. "Who even buys something like this here?"

Mom put the red knit atrocity in the shopping cart and answered her own question.

"He can wear it for our family picture," she said, reaching for the Dremel 4000 box.

"And have we come to a decision as to where that picture will be taken?"

Mom's eyes narrowed. "Your father is a stubborn man. He's still complaining about our tree. Says he's developed an allergy to it. But I don't care, it's staying."

Audria covered her mouth and laughed out loud.

"It's not funny. That man is a handful." Mom folded her arms. "But, I think we can both have our way with that picture."

"How? Standing in front of a Christmas tree on the front porch of the cabin?" A bit snarky, but Audria smiled at her own sarcasm.

"Actually..." Mom tapped her lip. "That's not a bad idea at--"

"I'm joking. Goodness."

Mom shrugged as if the idea were still something to be considered and eased the Dremel tool box into the cart. Shopping with Mom was like playing Tetris with a shopping cart--everything had to fit just right.

"Done." She swiped her hands. "We got a lot accomplished today."

Audria nodded and yawned. A full day called for a full cup of coffee right about now.

After packing the shoeboxes at Richland Middle for Maddox's unit, she and Mom mailed them off. Thirty boxes mailed overseas took quite a chunk of time, but it was time well spent.

"Let's see," Mom said. "We've been to the craft store, the thrift store, dollar store, anywhere else on our list?"

Audria smiled. Mom was the only person she knew who could spend a hundred dollars at the dollar store.

"That about covers it." Audria shook her head and thumbed through her mental 'things to get' list. Ribbon, wrapping paper--check. But she'd have to buy rolls of fleece later, or Mom would know for sure what she was making for her homemade Christmas gifts.

"Look at us go, and it's not even dinner time."

They headed toward the check out, Audria's mind straying back to Quinton. She prayed for his safety and for the safety of Maddox and the other soldiers.

Perhaps if she had prayed more often for Clay, he'd still be here. She winced, the thought cutting deep. It wasn't true; it wasn't true at all. God didn't work that way, but how God worked was beyond her. Why some lived, why others didn't.

"You're quiet all of the sudden."

Audria tucked her hair behind her ears and fiddled with the scarf around her neck. It was best to keep quiet when Mom pried.

"Don't think I didn't notice how you held on to that one particular package at the post office."

Audria managed to remain quiet.

"And don't think I haven't talked to Maddox and Nora--"

"Mom, I'm an adult."

"And I'm your Mom." They stood in line behind a couple whose cart was filled with Christmas lights.

Audria kept silent and scanned the candy bar selections to her right and left. Better to say nothing. Telling her about Quinton when there really was nothing to tell made no sense.

"From my sources..." Mom started.

Audria huffed. As if she didn't know who those sources were.

Mom continued, "The young man coming with Maddox to the cabin is head-over-heels for you."

Audria sighed and settled on a Kit Kat bar. She plucked it from its box and pointed it at Mom. "His name is Quinton, and we're just friends. We barely know each other."

"Okay, dear."

"Friends, Mom. That's. All."

"If you say."

"I do say."

"Then, okay."

The Christmas-light couple in front of them glanced over their shoulders. Audria offered a smile, and they turned. Could this line go any slower?

"What's he like?"

"Mom." Audria groaned, but conceded. "He's, well, he's really great."

"Easy to talk to?"

She nodded. Very easy. And so, so...warm and caring.

How dumb was it to have feelings for someone she'd never met and barely knew? But still...

"We haven't talked a whole lot. Several messages back and forth." Audria turned the Kit Kat over in her palms and toyed with the edge of the wrapping. "But, kind of hoping he'll call again." She couldn't hide her grin, and to be honest, she didn't want to.

Mom's eyes danced. "I'm glad you have a friend that can make you smile like that."

"Me, too."

"I can't wait to meet this young man."

Her heart went two directions, one wanting to leap, the other shouting words of caution. Neither side wrong, but which was right?

Mom gave her elbow a squeeze. "I just wish Maddox and Quinton would be home for Christmas."

"Me, too." Both sides of her heart were in agreement there. Everyone deserved to come home for Christmas.

***

Rolls of Buffalo plaid fleece splayed around her. Audria sat on her apartment floor in her most comfortable sweats, back pressed against the couch. She admired the lovely fleece pattern, a bold Christmas red with wide black overlaying stripes she'd chosen for the top.

Underneath, she'd picked a thick solid black fleece with rivets that created a humming effect on her palm when she rubbed her hand over top.

Together, both patterns oozed of cozy, comfort, Christmas, and the perfect homemade gift for her family.

A prayer blanket for each of them. Quinton, too.

The two portions of fleece would be tethered together with many knots, each knot representing a prayer said on their behalf. Beautiful in thought, but she prayed she had the talent to get it done.

Audria leaned, balancing on her knees as she hovered over the material to measure. Not too long, but no too short. The Pinterest directions said 66x90. What was that in yards? She closed her eyes to start the whole division process, but all those numbers, yuck. Instead, she relied on her phone calculator. Such a lifesaver.

Sort of. What was with all these decimals?

She scribbled on paper and then sighed. Her blanket would be rounded to the nearest number in yards. And that would be--

Her phone rang.

Audria finished writing down her measurement and grinned. Quinton.

"Hello," she said.

"Hi." He sounded...good.

"I'm, I'm glad you called."

"I would've called sooner, but there's that whole time difference here and everything."

"I get it." She rocked back on her heels and sat, moving a pile of fleece to the side.

"I got your messages. Thank you, and I guess I'm okay with Netflix and chick-flicks."

She laughed. "How are things?"

"Pretty uneventful, but I'll take that over the alternative."

"I bet."

"We do have a pretty mean puzzle going, though."

"Um?"

"Gotta pass the time somehow. Today it's puzzles, tomorrow probably weightlifting. Keeps us busy 'til the next mission. How about you? Anything new?"

"Mom and I went shopping today." Had Maddox told him about the care packages? Maybe that was supposed to be a surprise. Audria kept that quiet. "Grabbed dinner, and now I'm sitting here making Christmas gifts."

"About that..."

"Maddox just told you, didn't he? What a jerk."

"It's okay."

"You're totally exempt from making gifts, really. Actually, you don't have to bring any gifts."

"That's not going to happen."

"Still."

"So, how does this whole gift thing work? Do you make something for everyone? That could get more expensive than actually buying something."

"We do make a gift for everyone, but it's just the four of us. We don't really see extended family much since they're far away, so we send them gift cards." She pulled a pillow from the couch and placed it under her stomach and wiggled until comfortable. "But making gifts, yeah, it can get pricey, but we are thrifty people. For the most part. Though Mom splurged on a crazy tool to make Dad's gift."

He laughed, and the phone line rattled. "I think it's a cool idea, just...different."

"We've always been okay with being a little different."

"It's one of the things I like about you. One of the many."

Her face warmed, a reply she was grateful he couldn't

see.

"I'm sorry," he said. "That was too forward. We're just getting to know each other."

"It's okay, but seriously, don't worry about the gifts. You're our guest." *Our* guest? Maddox's guest. Audria covered her face and rolled to her side.

"I learned something new about you."

She propped herself up with an elbow. "Go on."

"You have a nickname."

"No. No." She smacked her forehead. "I'm going to kill Maddox."

"I'm not sure if I even want to know how you earned a name like 'Tooter.'"

"Ick. I can't. We'll never be friends again. Ugh. Let's just say it involves the quietest moment at church possible and the reason I no longer eat Cajun-spicy food. Mexican, I'm cool with. Cajun? No."

"Oh. Wow." Quinton chuckled, and she laughed along.

"Yeah. I was thirteen. And sitting beside the guy I liked. Seventh grade was awful, but after that, I begged Mom and Dad to send me away or become Amish." They did neither.

If a body could grimace, hers was right now, simply recalling the devastating event.

"I'm trying so hard, but--" Quinton sputtered, clearly attempting not to laugh.

"It's funny, just not funny when it happens to you, and I pray it never does. But this isn't fair." Audria smacked at the carpet and grinned. "You have to tell me something horrendously embarrassing now that you know my worst moment ever."

"I'm not sure that's how it works."

"It's totally how this works."

"In that case," he said, still chuckling. "My junior year

of high school, I worked at a toy store during the Christmas season. Crazy busy."

"I bet." She imagined him working behind a register or stocking shelves.

"My feet hurt. Customers were nuts. All I wanted to do was get home and play video games."

"Typical teen guy stuff."

"This woman came in with a stroller. Cute baby, didn't think anything of it. When I was ringing up her items, she started talking to me and telling about her baby, and I, I must've not been thinking clearly, 'cause I said," he laughed. "I asked if she was having another baby."

Audria gasped. "You did not!"

"I didn't mean it like that, it's just, you know, she still had some baby weight, and I opened my dumb mouth."

"Oh. My. Gosh."

"I know. It was terrible. She threw the toys at me, called me a jerk, and asked to speak to my manager." He drew in a breath. "I prayed I'd never run into her again, but I swear she came in all of the time after that. Always gave me an evil eye."

"They didn't fire you?"

"Nope, but I ran into some trouble outside of school and work, and well, the rest is history. Ended up joining the Army after high school graduation."

"You were enlisted before becoming an officer?"

"Eight years."

"What?"

"Yup. True story. Made it to a Staff Sergeant, finished my degree and got my commission five years ago."

"I had no clue."

"I think it makes me a better leader, you know? Having experience in both the enlisted and officer worlds."

"Completely agree." Could this man be any more impressive? Audria found herself twirling a piece of her hair and stopped. "So, you were homeless, and now look at you."

"It's by the grace of God."

"Wow."

"When I came off the streets, Dad was happy to welcome me home, but I wasn't willing to patch things up yet." Quinton sighed, and her heart ached listening to him recall such a difficult time in his life. "It wasn't until I graduated college that I really reached out to him."

"What made you want to reconnect?"

Quinton release a short laugh. "I didn't want to be at graduation alone."

Audria lifted her brows. "Well, whatever works."

"Now, we're good, but I so wish I could take back how I treated him."

"I'm sure he knows that."

"He does, and he was super proud when I graduated."

"What did you get your degree in?"

"Math."

"Ugh. I was just fighting with my calculator before you called." Audria flipped to her back and lifted her legs, resting her ankles on the couch cushion. "Why math?"

"Figured it was versatile. Whenever I get out of the Army, want to keep my options open."

"Smart." She reached for a piece of fleece and rolled it between her fingers. "Do you mind me asking about some of the trouble you got in before you joined?"

Quinton sighed. "I don't mind, but please don't think I'm still that way."

"Not at all, it's just, there's this kid at a school where my best friend is the principal, and I'm worried about him and his family. Thought maybe you could give me some insight."

"Fill me in, and I'm happy to help."

Audria told him about Jayce, the two jobs his mother worked, how they were struggling to make life work, and how Jayce seemed to be on the cusp of going the wrong way.

"Wow, yeah, that's a tough one," he said.

Audria rested a palm on her head. "I don't know how to help, and giving them a shoebox filled with things isn't nearly enough."

"Why do you feel like you need to solve this?"

She paused and worked not to take offense. "It's my job."

"I'm not trying to be disrespectful. Just want to understand." His tone was calm, and hers apparently wasn't.

"I'm sorry, I...I guess I feel responsible. Sometimes shoeboxes don't seem like enough." And they weren't. But they were something. "There are things that I can't help with. Outcomes I can't change, but when I can, I want to. I have to."

"Do you think the pull you feel to make a difference in the outcome, maybe, well, it might be connected to losing Clay?"

Her ears rang, and her throat constricted. Tears bit the corner of her eyes.

"I'm sorry, Audria, that was too personal. I overstepped."

"You did." She sat and pulled her knees to her chest. "But I don't think you're wrong."

She couldn't control the outcome--Clay had died. But she could control some things, like where her time and money went, and who she could help.

Audria closed her eyes. "Can we focus on Jayce and

his family for now?"

"Sure. I'm so sorry. Let's, um, let's forget I ever said that."

A steady stream of tears flowed down her cheeks. She wiped them away with the corner of her sleeve.

"Let's think about the things that you can control in this situation," he said.

She nodded, brain suddenly full. "I'm not sure."

"Well, we know what you can't control. You can't control the choices Jayce makes, but think about things they need and the resources or maybe contacts you have that might be able to assist. And maybe that help will influence his decisions in a good way. He'll see another path."

"You're right." Perhaps the help would positively influence him, or allow him the freedom to choose better. "I have resources."

A sea of them. Most remained untapped because people didn't know about them.

Audria scratched her head, eyes still closed. "I keep thinking we help students succeed when we help their families succeed. I just don't know how I'd physically be able to connect all these families with helpful resources. I'm the only Homeless Liaison in the district."

"What if you could streamline the process for them to get help? Like host some sort of an event."

"An event?"

"Maybe kind of like speed dating, but with companies or people or churches able and willing to help."

Audria stood, thumbnail locked between her front teeth. "Families could go to the booths they were interested in. Speak with the people in charge face to face. A booth for school supplies, clothing, housing, hot meals." Her mind raced. "Oh, my gosh. Genius."

Quinton laughed.

She paced the room, one hand on top of her head. "How do we get them there? Where do I start?"

"That's one thing I know you'll be able to figure out."

Yes, she would.

Chapter Nine

THE DAYS BLURRED by. So much to do. So much to plan.

Audria rolled back in her desk chair and plucked a candy cane from her candy stash while browsing over her work calendar.

How was it already Thursday the 19th?

Thankfully, with a bit of coffee, she had finished the final of the four prayer blankets last night, careful to take time each day to make sure every knot was represented by a prayer. And goodness, after about the tenth knot, her prayers got a bit creative. Hopefully, God didn't mind that.

Tomorrow was the last day before Christmas break. Saturday was the town's Christmas Parade. And after the parade, the event she'd spent nearly every moment planning since Quinton so brilliantly suggested it.

They had decided on a name--Resource Rotation. Okay, so not the most glamorous name, but it worked. And truly, it hadn't been difficult to pull together. All the churches, businesses, and nonprofits already helping in many ways agreed to come together in one location for an evening like no other. The city bus system offered to supply transportation to anyone wanting to come. Just amazing.

Mom and her Bunco Babes agreed to serve refreshments, and Dad offered to set up a live Christmas tree, but Mom caught on to his ploy to rid their house of their living tree. Yesterday, Audria personally invited Jayce's mom, Ms. Dickens, to attend. The woman cried and held on to her.

God was so good to allow all the pieces to fall into place.

Audria grinned and dabbed at her eyes. Her heart hummed, no sang, and for the first time in two years she felt it, that hope Christmas brings. Audria wrapped her infinity scarf around her neck and waved to her coworkers. Time for her morning rounds.

She checked her phone for any missed messages. Nothing yet. Audria twisted her lips to the side. He'd call or message.

The RV started with a roar, and with a few sputters, she was off to Richland Middle for most of the day. Loading up and delivering the boxes to students unable to pick them up would take time. About a hundred of those this year. Thankfully, Nora promised to help. Mom and Dad wanted to take part, too. Between the four of them, they could knock this task out by tomorrow for sure.

Twenty-five homes each meant about twelve each day. Ha. Audria bobbed her head. *Look at me doing math.*

Quinton would be proud.

Her phone jingled. A Facetime call from Nora. Audria mounted her phone on the dashboard stand and swiped to answer.

"Hey, girl." Nora waved. "How's it feel to be Monday night's bronze star trivia winners?"

"Your hair, wow."

"Added a little Christmas red. You know me, got to be festive."

Yes, she did. "I'll admit, third place isn't bad. We make a great team."

And the topics were more on their level. Disney movies and 'name that song.'"

Nora held up a medal.

Audria squinted. "Are you seriously wearing that at school? It's from Dos Amigos."

"The students don't know that. They just see a winner."

Audria laughed and rolled her eyes. "Hey, I'm on my way."

Nora's eyes darted. "Hold on a minute."

"Are you hiding in your office again?"

"Don't judge me, and no, I'm not. I've got this teacher drama going on, and if they come in my office one more time arguing over who should've won the door decorating contest, I might fire both of them."

"I'm so glad I don't have your job."

"And I'm glad I don't have yours, 'cause all those kids wouldn't be getting shoeboxes."

"Yes, they would. You have a big heart."

Nora rolled her eyes but smiled.

"Any word on Jayce? Teachers noticing a difference?"

She twisted her lips for a second. "Sort of. Thanks to the city bus pass, his attendance has improved. Grades are iffy, but they said he's a bit more pleasant."

"That's a start. I'll take it." Audria nodded. Even the smallest victories should be celebrated. "You sure you're able to come with me today and tomorrow?"

"Girl, why do you think I have a vice principal? He gets paid to fill in for me when I'm out on important missions. Speaking of missions, I hear yours is going well."

"You mean the Resource Rotation event? Yeah, I'm so excited--"

"I mean Quinton." Nora's face scrunched, her lips twisted into a pinch. "How's it going?"

Audria frowned and shook her head. She kept her eyes on the road. "It's good."

"And that's all you're giving me? And you wonder why I have to get all my details from Maddox."

"Maddox doesn't know near as much as he thinks he does."

"He knows a lot more than you think, and I know something you don't. It's a surprise."

"You are seriously a child."

"That's why you love me."

True. Nora was gold.

"I think you're gonna like it."

"I'm sure." What in the world was Maddox up to? Surely some kind of crazy homemade gift. Like the ugly Christmas sweater he pieced together with cat images all over it. Ick.

Nora giggled. "Anyway, hey, I'm totally cool with delivering these boxes, but I'm gonna have to be home tonight by seven. Marcus and I have a hot date."

"Boo. I was hoping we could catch a movie. I still have the money Maddox sent me. Two free movies on him. Whoop, whoop." Audria did a dance in her seat, and the RV rocked side to side.

"Girl, you save that money and take Mr. Quinton when you get to the cabin."

"Um, first off, we're not going on a date, and second, if we were, then I wouldn't be paying."

"That's right, Maddox would be."

Audria laughed and nearly ran a red light.

"When are all of you leaving for the cabin?"

"Sunday after church. We'll stay through New Year's."

"I keep telling Marcus we have got to join y'all one year."

"The more the merrier." At least that's what her family seemed to think. She, however, remained undecided.

"We're visiting his family in Chicago, but next year for sure. Hey, so, before I forget, I'd like to ask you something."

Audria braced herself.

"Don't make that face. Geez." Nora snapped her fingers, just as Audria went over a speed bump a bit too fast. "I was talking with the kids in the Junior Service Club. You know what an honor it is to be chosen to be Randall the Raideer in the town's Christmas parade."

Audria nodded. A strange honor, but yes, the students coveted the one chosen to be Randall the Raideer in the Christmas parade.

"The kids vote every year, and this year, they didn't vote for a student, they voted for you." Nora grinned, eyes wide.

"What?" Audria physically felt her face droop. Speechless didn't begin to describe it. "You want me to dress up like Randall the Rudolph Red-Nosed Raideer Reindeer?"

That was a mouthful.

Nora nodded, grin still wide.

"You want...me? To walk around like dressed like...that?"

"It's an honor."

"Why me?"

"The kids and the whole school have been moved by your selfless service to others."

Ugh. Geez. That was so sweet, but... "Can't they get me a gift card?"

"Audria Rylatt, this is a position these students fight over, and here you are complain--"

"All right, all right. I'll do it." Audria signaled left and braked.

"They're going to be so happy. This will be amazing."

Or not. "Hey, I'm pulling into the parking lot."

Audria ended the call and parked.

Forget the reason behind her nickname 'Tooter,' now her most embarrassing moment may become frolicking in a souped up reindeer costume in front of the town.

At least it was for a good cause. Ugh. What in the world was she getting herself into?

Chapter Ten

WEIGHTS CLINKED, SOME clattered, and a few soldiers heckled one another while scribbling down their victories on a clipboard.

Quinton laughed and spotted the youngest soldier. "Don't let the bar touch your neck. Aim for your chest."

The boy-like soldier nodded, face reddened and strained.

"C'mon," Quinton said. "You got this. Steady. Steady."

The boy's arms shook. A crowd gathered. Bets were placed. Some fist bumped while others frowned shaking their heads, but Quinton focused on the soldier. Of course, this kid had put on weights too heavy for him to lift. Male bravado was a curious thing.

"Focus. Breathe." Quinton modeled his breathing and waited for the boy to follow. "There you go, now lift."

Two veins protruded from the young soldier's forehead. He grunted, eyes clamped shut, and the others laughed and jeered.

"Ignore them and lift." At some point, lifting became a mindset, choosing to push past the pain to do the impossible.

The young soldier drew in a strong breath, chest rising. He gritted his teeth, eyes narrowed, and pushed. A guttural groan lurched from his mouth as his arms lifted the bar. He did it. The bar clanked to a resting position, and the soldier leapt from the bench with an 'I told you I could do it' grin.

Quinton slapped the young soldier's back, their hands smacking into a quick slide shake before folding into a half hug. A blend of cheers and sighs and 'pay-ups' filled the space. All in good fun.

The weight room was more than weights. These guys were family, and this space was where they could hang loose, especially on days like this--when spirits were high. Most were going on leave. Most of them, including himself, would be on their way home within the next twenty-four hours. In his case, he boarded a plane in six hours and, Quinton eyed his watch, twenty-two minutes.

"Hey, Captain Nolan," the young soldier called out. "Let's see how many pull-ups you can do."

Quinton turned and grinned. "I'll put all of you to shame."

A few soldiers near the pull-up bar pointed to the clipboard on the wall, and Quinton bobbed his head. "My name's still on top of that list. Let me know when you beat it."

A few 'ooh's,' 'roasted,' and laughs followed suit. Quinton rubbed his hands together and walked past the Christmas tree near the row machine. He wormed his way around the three bum couches angled in front of a good-sized plasma TV. An old foosball table hung out behind the farthest couch, and a few long tables stood sporadically about the room. A game of poker carried on at one table, a large unfinished puzzle at another, and the last sat stacked with board games.

Nothing fancy, but the rec/weight room was often better than sitting in one's bunk. He rounded the corner.

"Where you going?" Major Rylatt said, arms filled with brown wrapped boxes each, tied with festive red ribbon. "Can you give me... a...hand?" His voiced strained.

"Sure." Quinton took several of the boxes. "Where you want these?"

"Under the tree. They've got names on them. Here, take the rest." Major Rylatt plopped the remaining boxes in Quinton's arms.

"Um, sir, I need to make a quick call to my dad before I start getting ready to leave."

"It won't take long. Besides--" Major Rylatt turned. "One of those boxes is for you, from someone pretty special."

Did he just wink? Quinton shook his head and ambled back into the weight room, careful to set each box beneath the tree. Which one had his name on it?

Quinton search, but nothing yet.

"I've got one more load." Major Rylatt knelt and placed the boxes. "Here. This is what you're looking for."

Quinton took the box and turned it over in his hands. "Who are all of these from?"

"Me," Major Rylatt said. He lifted his chest and outstretched his arms. "Merry Christmas everyone. Come find your box."

"These are from you?" Quinton scratched his head as a swarm of soldiers rushed the tree. "You said it was from someone special, and then you winked at me. Kind of makes a fella wonder..."

"Fine. It's actually from Audria."

"Audria?"

"It was my idea, and she put them all together."
"And she picked me to make a box for?"
"Something like that."
"Uh-huh." Sounded like some sort of conspiracy.
"Don't ask questions. Just go with it." Major Rylatt folded his arms. "I've got to go get the remaining boxes."

"Need help, sir?"

"Nope. Enjoy your Christmas present."

"Whatever you say, sir." Quinton held the box and ran a thumb over her writing. So neat and feminine, unlike his barely legible scribble. Did she really make his...special? The thought made his heart thump to the rhythm of an unfamiliar cadence.

He'd be stateside within twenty-four hours.

He'd see her face to face. At the town Christmas parade. A surprise meeting, Major Rylatt suggested. An idea that seemed fun and even romantic only days ago, but now?

Quinton swallowed and stood.

Did she even want to meet him?

Did she even want to send him a box?

Or was all of this orchestrated by meddling friends and family?

"You all right?"

Quinton lifted his head to see the young soldier he'd helped spot minutes ago. He nodded. "Relationship stuff."

"Ignore them and lift."

"Come again?"

"That's what you told me. 'Ignore them and lift.'"

"How does that help me right now?"

"You look stressed. Like you're worried about this relationship."

"And?" Was this kid some sort of a mind reader?

"So, ignore them--those doubts, and lift--just go for

it."

That was simple. But complicated.

Quinton cradled the gift under one arm. "Ignore them and lift."

"That's right. I mean, you'll never know if you don't go for it."

"You're pretty smart for a private."

"Naw." The young soldier shrugged. "I just know when I've been given some good advice."

Quinton shook the soldier's hand and held up the gift. "Guess I'm gonna go ignore them and lift."

***

Quinton scooted his duffle bag to the edge of the cot. He didn't have much to pack, so it could wait. Right now, that gift kept calling his name.

The ribbon untied with ease. A wave of rich chocolate, sugar, peanut butter, and peppermint reached past the tissue paper and danced on the tip of his nose. The scent brought a smile to his face as he pushed past the glittered tissue paper. His hand brushed against a sharp corner--a red envelope.

He plucked the card from the package.

Merry Christmas, Quinton,

Surprise!

It seems like my brother is good at pulling off such things, and usually I do my best to avoid his shenanigans, but I'm definitely on board with this one. It's been an honor to send a bit of Christmas, even if it's in a box, to all of you serving so far from home. Thank you for your service and sacrifice.

I've enjoyed getting to know you, and have come to cherish our friendship.

Did she still see him as only a friend? His heart sank a bit.

While I do believe we have a few people meddling in our lives, I will say, they're right about how incredible you are. I am actually looking forward to meeting you around New Years.

So much sooner. Quinton smiled and continued reading.

I pray for your safety, and for the safety of all of the soldiers. I cannot imagine being away from home on Christmas, and though this gift cannot replace all the comforts and joys of Christmastime with family and friends, I pray that it brings you some comfort and some joy. If anything, I hope that it appeases your sweet tooth, or sweet teeth.

Hugs,
   Audria

Quinton tapped the letter against his knee.
　　She prayed for him. She prayed for his soldiers.
　　She prayed.
　　The woman was love in action. She loved God and others with the way she lived her life.
　　He smiled and dug through the contents of the box.
　　Candy canes.
　　Containers of crunchy peanut butter. *Score.* She remembered.
　　Hygiene products. Deodorant and toothpaste were always a good thing.
　　More candy. *Awesome.*
　　A Christmas-themed country cabin puzzle. He laughed.
　　Air fresheners. *Ha.* It's like she knew how bad a bunch of soldiers smelled.
　　Protein Powder. *Wow. Not bad at all.*
　　And...Quinton continued to dig, pushing the candy

aside.

Macarons. He paused and eased the gems from the box as if defusing a bomb. She put them in their own Christmas-themed container. Twelve of them. Chocolate. With...he sniffed. Not simply chocolate, but almost like hot chocolate. His mouth watered.

Quinton lifted one from its place and bit.

A flakey, sugary experience that melted on impact.

It was hot chocolate.

The center was creamy. Ganache he believed is what she called it. Definitely milk chocolate, but with a hint of toasted marshmallow.

Insane amazing. How did she do it?

Quinton bobbed his head and picked up another. One more, then pack. Pack and call Dad.

He chewed, snatched up another and packed his duffle bag. Aside from a few pair of gyms shorts and white T's, most of his clothes were military. Definitely needed to go shopping or stop by his apartment once he got back to Ft. Campbell.

If he was meeting Audria at the town Christmas parade, he'd need to look and smell a whole lot nicer than he did currently.

Quinton rolled the last of his clothing items, shoved them into the bag, and dialed his dad.

Long distance calls took a while to go through. Though, he was closer to his father here in Afghanistan than when he was stateside.

"Hey, Son." His dad's voice brought a smile to Quinton's face.

"Dad, how are you?"

"Eating right now, so I'm pretty good."

Quinton grimaced. Indian food wasn't his favorite, but the bread, *naan*, was delicious.

"More importantly, Son, how are you?"

"Headed home."

Dad groaned and sighed. "I wish we could be together for Christmas this year."

"Don't beat yourself up, Dad. You're right where God wants you to be, and so am I."

"You could always fly down here."

"I'd love to, but I sort of have plans. With a friend." Was his voice unsteady?

Quinton cleared his throat.

"Yeah?"

"He invited me to spend Christmas with...um...his...family."

"So, there's a girl involved."

"What? How did you? I didn't say anything about a girl."

"Son, you don't have to say a word." Dad's chuckle rumbled through the phone. "I can hear it in your voice. Tell me about her."

"Her name's Audria."

"Audria. I like it."

"Dad, she's amazing. She's everything I've prayed for. She's everything Mom prayed for."

"She'd have to be an incredible woman to catch your eye."

"I think she's the one."

"Have you even met her yet?"

"That's the crazy part."

He laughed again. "A bit, but then again, who would've ever thought I'd be pastoring in India and you'd be talking about prayer? God works best in the crazy."

"Exactly. And it is crazy. I'm meeting her tomorrow night for the first time. I'm excited, nervous, terrified."

Dad's chuckle deepened, and Quinton could almost see him smacking his knee. "I felt the same way when I met your mother. That woman. Did I tell you about the gift I bought, well made for her? Gave it to her on our first date."

"You made Mom a gift?" Quinton listened close. He still needed a gift idea for Audria and the rest of her family.

"The necklace she always wore."

Impressive. It was a simple necklace. A single marble-looking stone. "How did you learn to do that?"

"I was a young soldier once, too, you know. When I was stationed in South Korea, I sometimes walked the streets on my time off. Watched vendors make things. When I met your mom back stateside, I figured she might appreciate something I handmade."

What was with the handmade gifts? They were sweet and all, but was he the only person on the planet not opposed to buying gifts from a store? Or a gift card?

He needed something unique, but lovely, like Audria. Something to fit within his limited crafting ability. Quinton bit at his thumbnail and tapped against his teeth.

His dad continued. "Your mom, she was...she was the best half of me. And oh, how she loved you."

Quinton fought against the tightness in his throat. "I still miss her."

"Me, too, Son. She'd be so proud of you and the man you've become."

He'd wondered that many times, given his past. His choices as a teen would have broken her heart. "I hope you're right, Dad."

"I know I am. God has worked miracles in your life. You are an answer to prayer."

Quinton nodded. Dad was right. God stepped in just in time. He paused, hand cupping his chin while his memory took him back to that dark alley years ago. He was seventeen...

"You there, Son?"

"Just thinking," Quinton said. He folded his arms and pressed his back against the wall. "I don't know if Audria feels the same about me."

"There's definitely risk involved with each relationship."

"She's already risked so much."

"How so?"

"Clay was her fiancé."

"I see." Dad sighed. "Then she does have a lot to risk."

"Yeah." Quinton drew in a solid breath and let it out with unease. Remembering fallen soldiers never got easier, especially those he considered a friend.

"Does she know he was your friend?"

"I'm sure she does." Didn't she? How could she not? Quinton pushed from the wall and paced before pausing. "Do you think that matters?"

"Oh, it matters. You haven't told her?"

"It never came up."

"Son, she needs to know, or you need to make sure she knows."

A slow heat climbed its way up his neck. Quinton rolled his head from side to side, easing the building tension. Dad was right, but what if it all went wrong?

Chapter Eleven

"I'M NOT GOING anywhere other than the Christmas parade dressed like this." Audria frowned into the full-length mirror, hands plopped at her sides. "I look hideous."

"It's not so bad, dear," Mom giggled. "I mean, sweetie."

"Nice use of the word 'dear'."

"Completely unintentional."

"Mmhmm."

Mom patted Audria's shoulder, failing to hide her grin. "I'm proud of you."

"I'm standing in a school bathroom dressed as...this thing."

"For a good cause. Now embrace it and make our town proud.

This town really needed to reevaluate the things that made them proud.

"Remember to turn your nose on."

Ugh. That flashing monstrosity.

"Thanks," Audria said through a groan.

Mom opened the door, and they were met with cheers of insane Randall fanatics. Students high-fived and shouted, donning their own red noses.

"Right this way," the parade director said as he ushered her out. "You look stunning."

Or stunned. But really, at this point, was there a difference?

"Take your place right...here." The director pointed to the front float in the parking lot. A flatbed trailer loaded with faux snow, a sparkling, twirling North Pole sign, and a sleigh. "You'll sit there."

The sleigh. Nice.

No Santa needed when Randall was in town. Audria smiled. Might as well try to have a bit of fun.

The director help her onto the float. Walking with fake hooves was no easy task.

"Looking snazzy, Tooter." Dad wormed his way to the side of the float.

She nodded a thanks and crossed her hooves. "Ready to get it over with."

"Your mom and I are filming this." He seemed pleased at the prospect. Something to watch over and over. Mortifying really. "We love you, Tooter. Go Raideers!" Dad held his belly and laughed.

"Thanks." She waved bye, wanting nothing more than for the whole thing to start or be over or both.

"Thank you for doing this." Nora climbed up and took a seat on the sleigh.

"This is totally for the kids."

"We have to tap out a bit early."

"You're not staying the whole time?" Audria's palms dampened. She rubbed them on the faux fur covering her knees.

Nora winced. "We'll be here for most, but we have to run to Nashville to pick up a few things. Christmas time, you know?" She waved a hand. "No worries. We'll be back for the Resource Rotation."

Audria gulped, and Nora patted her hand.

"You got this, girl," she said with such confidence Audria wanted to believe. "So, you, um, you brought a change of clothes, right?"

"Was I supposed to?"

"I sent you a text."

"I have hooves, Nora." She shook the flopping atrocities hanging from her hands. "I can't text right now or even answer my phone."

Nora stifled a giggle. "You will want to change."

"It's priority number one when this is over. Wait--" Audria lowered her shoulder leaning closer to Nora. "Why will I want to change? For the Resource Rotation, right?"

"Or--" Nora's face pinched. "For Maddox's surprise."

Maddox. Audria let the thought settle. "His surprise?"

Nora winced and nodded. "Keep going."

His surprise meant she needed to change. But what would he care unless... "Is he home?"

Nora's nod began slow, her eyes lighting up.

The instant joy was met with near instant fear. "Wait. That means. He's home?" Her head spun. "And that means..."

"There's a pretty good reason to change from your costume."

"Quinton's here, too?"

"That's right." She clapped her hands together and pulled Audria into a hug.

He wasn't coming home for another week or more.

No. No. No. Audria shook her head, frozen in Nora's grip. "Nora, I can't let him see me like this."

"He'll be just as proud as we all are."

Her stomach flipped. "I'm going to be sick."

"It's show time," shouted the parade director.

Nora slid from the sleigh. "You'll do great."

"Don't leave me like this."

A cold sweat prickled her skin beneath the costume. Oh, yes, this was indeed the most mortifying moment of her life.

***

The entire parade was a blur. A literal sick blur. Audria held to the side of the sleigh, inner-monologuing pep-talks most of the way, and waved to the cheering blurs.

"This is for the children. The students," she whispered to herself in between waves. Her antlers bounced with each jolt of the float, and the red nose flickered on and off digging into the sides of her nostrils. "It's an honor. Yes, an honor."

Down the alleys, narrow streets, and side roads she stayed focused, head lowered as much as possible.

No eye contact. Just waving. Waving and keeping her mouth clamped closed to keep her stomach from holding an uprising that would surely make front page news.

'Randall the Rudolph Raideer Reindeer vomits on adoring fans.'

Not something she needed stuck to her name.

And how long did this town Christmas parade last?

Too long.

At least she hadn't spotted Dad with the camera, or Maddox, or...Quinton.

Audria gulped and attempted a smile for the crowd. The float jostled along, not helping to ease her uneasy nerves. After an eternity, the float made its way back to the middle school parking lot, greeted by the director and a host of others she had no intention of talking to.

"Way to go, Tooter." Dad was the first to reach the

float. He stretched out his arms to help her down.

Audria hurried. "I've got to go."

"Where?"

Anywhere but here, in this outfit. "Dad, please, I...I've got to leave--"

"But we've got a surprise for you."

Is that what a death sentence is, a surprise?

"I'll meet you guys at the Resource Rotation. I really need to change fir--"

"Hey, Sis." She'd know that voice anywhere. Audria stood, feet cemented, back turned.

Oh, Lord, please, no. Not now. She shut her eyes and prayed until she saw spots.

Slowly, she turned and opened one eye just to be certain.

Yup, Maddox was home, and all smiles.

And to his side stood Quinton.

Audria lifted a hand, or rather, a hoof, and waved.

I'm going to die.

Chapter Twelve

U̲n̲l̲e̲s̲s̲ s̲h̲e̲ h̲i̲d̲ behind the Christmas tree, there was no place in this room Audria could hide. At least she'd been able to change out of that ridiculous deer costume. The look on Quinton's face. Ick. But it was over, and life continued. In fact, lots of life, the good kind, was happening right now.

Audria gave a nod, chin high. The Resource Rotation was in full swing. Christmas music filled the room, adding to the festive ambiance. Dad played Santa and surprisingly, he played the part well, taking time to listen to each child's wishes. Mom and her Bunco Babes manned the snack table, helping the younger children create the cutest edible creations. Snowmen from marshmallows and pretzels. Strawberries coated with green tinted white chocolate perched on top of a crisp cookie made an adorable Christmas tree scene.

Maddox even took part reading stories to the children. Quinton worked alongside helping students select books to take home. Hundreds were donated from the library.

She tried not to stare, but the way he knelt and focused on each student...

He looked up. Their eyes caught for a moment, and she turned, happy to find Nora waltzing her way.

"Girl, this is amazing." Nora opened her arms and pulled Audria in for a hug. "Cute outfit."

"It's nothing." That 'nothing' took trying on six shirts, two skirts, and three dresses before deciding on a hip red and black plaid button up, and fitted black slacks. One could only do so much within a thirty-minute time frame to change from G.I. Reindeer into a professional hosting a professional event.

"It's nothing? You're in heels. And you have lipstick on."

"I wear heels and lipstick."

"On Easter Sunday."

"Well, it's...never mind. I wanted to look nice."

"Wonder why?" Nora teased. "Anyway, sorry we're late."

"No worries."

"Nashville was just crazy."

"On the Saturday before Christmas, yes. I can't believe you went."

"Believe me. I talked to Jesus the whole time we were at the Opry Mills Mall. People are just plain rude, acting all ugly. Had to teach a few ladies some manners. And that traffic." She rolled her eyes and huffed. "Never again. Nope. Not doing Nashville at Christmastime anymore. I almost lost my faith."

"Oh, my word, woman." Audria shook her head.

"Anyway, this place looks fantastic, but I call dibs on decorating for next year." She stepped back, turning around and taking in the surroundings. "Did the church charge you to use this facility?"

"No way."

"Good 'cause I was about to find our pastor and give him a piece or two of my mind."

And Nora would. Audria laughed and wrapped an arm over Nora's shoulder.

"Girl, just look at all of this."

Audria smiled. *Yes, look at it.*

Stations lined the walls, each table representing a resource ready to connect and help families. Childcare, clothing, food, tutoring, extracurricular activities, transportation, resumé writing, Internet access, and more. So much more.

There were games for the children. Crafts. Music. Dancing. Toys.

Gifts for each family to take home.

And they were coming. Families lined up at the door and entering. Entering with smiles, traces of wonder, and relief painted their faces.

Was that Jayce's family coming through the door? Audria stood on her tippy toes, careful not to twist an ankle in her heels.

It was. They came! Her heart swelled. She waved to Jayce's mother, and the woman waved back, baby in one arm and Jayce at her side. *Thank you, Lord. Thank you.*

The room buzzed with a fresh excitement that surpassed holiday cheer.

Her lip trembled. "This is really happening."

Helping families meant helping students. Helping students meant helping the future. Forget test scores. And grades never went on a tombstone.

"No crying. Not tonight. Not yet," Nora said with a wave of her index finger. "You've got a man over there eyeing you--"

"Please." Audria placed a hand on her hip.

"Don't even act like you haven't been looking at him, too," Nora said with a snap. "Anyway. Marcus and I came to help. What can we do?"

"Make sure each family has a clipboard with the service provider checklist. Help them find the tables they are looking for and really, that's it."

"Got it. Clipboard with the checklist, help 'em find the table. What do they do when they're finished?"

"Oh, um, they'll meet with one of our pastors and counselors before heading out."

"That's wonderful."

"I thought so, too. Our church was so on board with this and wants to help plan for next year."

"Girl, that's wonderful news."

"I can't believe any of this is happening, and it's all because of...Quinton." His name was a whisper on her lips. Her eyes focused past Nora until they found him. That grin.

"I see that look on your face."

Audria lowered her gaze. "I don't even really know him, Nora."

"You know the important stuff. Give the rest time."

"It hurts."

Nora clasped Audria's hand between hers. "Clay loved you. And you loved Clay."

"I still love Clay."

"There's nothing wrong with that, but allowing yourself permission or the opportunity to love again is not wrong. It's not cheating on Clay, it's not dishonoring him."

"I know you're right..." Tears stung her eyes. She nodded and blinked them away.

"I'm not saying you have to marry Quinton, or if he's even 'the one,' but I am saying it's okay to be open to the possibility."

Open. Yes. She was open. And he was here. Here and helping.

"I better get to my job. No telling what Marcus will be having these folks doing if I don't get to him soon." Nora offered a smile and squeezed Audria's hand.

"Thank you." Audria returned the smile. "I'll be floating about if you need me."

"Looks like you aren't the only one floating." Nora grinned and pointed. "He's on his way over. Bye."

Audria reached for Nora's arm, but Nora evaded the hold and was on her way.

She swallowed and fidgeted with her hands, praying, hoping for someone, something, even a natural disaster to intervene at this point. Her heart did that thing again, lunging in opposite directions.

Be open.

It was one thing to chat on the phone, mail, and message online from a safe distance of thousands of miles, and something entirely different to be face to face.

Be open.

"Hi." He winced, head tilted, a shy grin growing on his face.

That face. That skin. Those eyes--a caramel color. Her heart stuck in her throat. Where was her voice?

"Hi," she said, tucking her hair behind her ears. Heat inched its way up her neck, and Audria was thankful for her collared shirt.

"This, this is all unbelievable." He scanned the room, hands digging into the pockets of his dark denim jeans. It paired nicely with the red V-neck sweater snug enough to reveal toned arms. Audria pried her eyes away.

"Thank you." She pressed her lips together. "It's because of you."

"No way." His smile grew, and her resolve faltered a bit more.

Be open.

"You put this together. I just, I just--"

"Came up with the idea."

He nodded. "Looks like we make a good team."

"Looks like it."

"Maddox said you delivered all of the Christmas shoeboxes to the kids who needed them? And pulled this event off? You're like some kind of superhero."

"I had a lot of help. Really, there's no way I could do any of this without all of the support."

"Well, it's incredible. You're incredible, and you must be tired."

Tired? Sleep. Ah, yes, her forgotten friend.

"Thank you, and yes, I am looking forward to some rest."

Perhaps the trip to the cabin was coming at the perfect time.

"And thank you," Quinton said.

"For?"

"The care package." His eyes widened. They sparkled. "It was...more than I ever imagined. And it really surprised me."

"Sometimes Maddox has good ideas." She swayed for a moment like some school-girl. "You're welcome."

"Those macarons...whew." He rubbed his stomach. "Wow."

"You ate them already? All of them?"

"And the crumbs."

Audria laughed. "That's a compliment."

"How long did it take you to make a dozen for each soldier?"

"Oh, um." Audria wet her lips. "Those were only for you...I...I wasn't sure, well, to be honest." She stumbled over her words, face warming. Why had she shown him such special treatment when putting together his gift? "I wanted to make yours special."

"Mission accomplished." He gave a slight nod.

"I guess I need a new mission now."

He grinned. "What kind? Something along the lines of skydiving?"

"Heavens, no." Audria put a palm over her heart. Although she couldn't say for certain, being here with him sure felt like skydiving. "I'm thinking something along the lines of simply being more open."

"A good start." He nodded, a slight grin growing on his handsome face. "It's really nice to finally meet you in person, Audria."

"You mean, when I'm not dressed like a Christmas-coated reindeer with ammo pouches and hooves?"

He laughed, head back. "Nah, nah, even then it was nice to meet you."

"Not my finest moment. I'd rather this be our first meeting."

"Okay then." He offered an extended hand. "Hello. My name is Quinton Nolan. It's a pleasure to meet you."

She placed her hand in his, surprised at the comfortable fit. "I'm Audria Rylatt, and it's a pleasure to meet you as well."

He held her hand a bit longer than necessary, but she took no offense.

***

Sunday service ended, and the Rylatt family plus one loaded their vehicles and headed east to Gatlinburg. The four-hour drive often turned into six. Restroom breaks for Mom's weak bladder, Perry's need to stretch his aged limbs, and Dad's affinity for gas station burritos were to thank for the added travel time. But the drive was always enjoyable. The scenery--exquisite. The conversation--hilarious.

"Georgie, remind me why we have our Christmas tree tied to the top of our vehicle."

"Jason, I don't want to buy another for the cabin."

"Then why in the world did we waste our time putting this thing up in the living room?"

"Time spent with our family is not wasted."

"Next year, I'm buying a fake tree for the cabin, and it can stay there."

"I've been asking you to do that for years, Jason."

The bantering between Mom and Dad truly needed to be recorded and sold.

Audria tuned them out and stretched her legs along the backseat. Perry grunted and rooted his way between her calves. He curled into a tighter ball and released a sigh. She rustled with his ears and turned her focus on the car coming up to their side. Maddox. Honking his horn and making dumb faces. Was he really an adult? An adult put in command of military men? The Army was filled with America's finest, yet she sometimes questioned their judgment. Quinton waved from the passenger side, and Audria smiled.

"He's a nice enough fella, Tooter" Dad said.

"They're just friends, dear," Mom answered before Audria could reply.

"He is nice, and yes, we're just friends."

Nestled in the arms of the great Smokey Mountains, Gatlinburg came into view with quaint shops bustling with life.

Audria cracked her window, and a flood of crisp air flooded her senses. Smells of taffy, caramel, and chocolate blended with fresh mountain air creating an aroma she'd wished for years to bottle and keep for herself.

Oh, this place.

"Georgie, I'm gonna have to stop soon."

"Jason, we are fifteen minutes from the cabin."

"I'm hungry," Dad said.

Audria and Perry shared a look, both knowing how

this would pan out.

"We've already stopped for groceries, and you've already had two burritos." Mom's tone quickened. Perry barked, and Mom shushed him. "You are simply going to have to wait, Jason."

"I didn't fight for this country so I could be told when I can and can't buy a burrito."

"Do you want me to call your heart doctor right now? 'Cause I will."

"Fine."

Audria kept a hand over her mouth to keep from laughing out loud. Maddox would roll when she told him. She pulled Perry onto her lap and rubbed around his ears until he began to doze. Soon, Gatlinburg faded, and the asphalt roads turned to gravel. They began to wind and curve upward, higher and higher until her ears popped. She yawned to relieve the pressure and watched as the evergreen trees grew thicker with each turn. Freshly fallen snow perched on their limbs. A cardinal darted low, his crimson feathers a delightful sharp contrast against the patches of snow. He followed along the car for no more than a heartbeat and then flew back to his home high in the treetops. She smiled and let the mountains welcome her back.

The family cabin peeked from its hill, the green roof laden with snow--a Christmas card scene come to life.

It had been two years since she'd seen this place. Two years since she let the hills hold her and speak solace to her soul. This was where she felt closest to God. Why had she stayed away? Why had she not drawn near?

Tension melted from her shoulders, the driest patches of her soul thirsted and craved the respite so near. Two years was too long.

So much had happened.

Parts of her had grown and mended...yet...not all.

But she was back, drawing near, and the thought was at once was both terrifying and exhilarating.

The cabin came into full view, and her body trembled.

Who knew what emotions awaited her? Could she face them?

Moments and memories bombarded her thoughts.

"We love you, Tooter." Dad reached back and gave her knee a quick pat. She smiled but kept quiet, thankful Mom didn't press.

Each turn of the tires brought her closer. Closer to her past but closer to moving forward.

Be open.

She nodded and released a slow breath.

Chapter Thirteen

"Maybe I shouldn't be here." Quinton sat in the passenger seat, car idling in the gravel drive. He watched Audria step from the backseat of the other car, both parents embracing her. She dabbed at her eyes and started up the cabin stairs.

Major Rylatt turned off the ignition. "She's okay."

"It doesn't look like it."

"This place holds a lot of memories for her. For all of us, really. And it's been hard. Clay was, well, you know. He was a great guy. And since losing him, her Christmas spirit wasn't the only thing Audria lost."

"I'm not able to fix what's broken in her. Only God can do that. So, if that's why you invited me, then I really shouldn't--"

"For one, I couldn't stand the thought of you staying back at Campbell alone. Christmas alone is depressing."

"I could've visited my Dad."

Major Rylatt continued, "Two, we're friends, even if I am your boss, so please call me Maddox until we get back to Afghanistan, and three--" He held up three fingers. "Well, you're the kind of guy who should be with my sister."

"But we're just friends right now."

"You and I both know there's more. There's something there."

"We just met. I don't even know where I stand with her."

"At least you stand."

"What does that mean?"

"She's been talking to you for a month now. You stand at least somewhere with her."

Somewhere was somewhere and not nowhere, and that was good. Right?

"I mean, I haven't seen her smile in a long time. A real smile."

"That's because--"

"Yes, she's awesome and is the most selfless and caring person I know. But I know her. I know she's been scared to love again, but you, well, you woke something inside of her."

Quinton shook his head. "How long do you think it will take her? To see that maybe she and I could be more?"

"You in a hurry?"

"I'd wait a lifetime for her."

"Let's pray it doesn't take that long."

"Just focus and lift."

"What?"

"Giving myself a little pep talk."

"C'mon." Major Rylatt slugged Quinton in the shoulder. "Let's get our stuff and help Dad drag the Christmas tree inside."

Quinton agreed but couldn't deny the hesitation that kept him hanging on to the door handle. Not a hesitation on his behalf but Audria's. He watched her dry her eyes and walk the length of the wrap-around porch, face solemn as her gaze fixed on something he could not tell. From this angle, she seemed to struggle. The last thing he wanted to do was push, pry, break her heart, or be the cause of anymore struggle.

***

The tree was up but bare. Something told Quinton Mrs. Rylatt would make certain every branch held some kind of decoration. It stood beside the nicest looking creek rock fireplace he'd ever seen. In fact, this might be the nicest cabin he'd ever seen. Not that he'd ever set foot in one.

Wood walls. Wood everything. Cedar or pine maybe? With the lighter shade and dark knots marking the logs, he'd guess pine. The open floor plan was nice. Kitchen, dining, and living area blended, giving the place a sense of family. A long craftsman style table joined the dining and living spaces together, and he imagined their family conversations were a bit livelier than others.

Tall windows on the first and second floors let in loads of light, and the view, wow. An airy smoke-like fog hovered over the tree tops. He could see for miles and for the first time, Quinton understood why someone would want to hideaway here. The mountains of Afghanistan were admittedly striking, but as a soldier in combat, they were equally dangerous--able to aide and hide the enemy. But here, the mountains were calm.

Quinton stepped back and took in the rest of his surroundings. A stairwell off to the side of the living room led to a large landing. From this view, he could see a few chairs, TV, and three doors.

Overhead, the ceiling formed a perfect peak. Quinton admired the large beams and the craftsmanship.

"It's impressive, huh?"

Quinton turned to find Mr. Rylatt watching him

intently. He swallowed to find his voice. "Yes, sir. Very impressive."

Audria's father had that Army retiree appearance written all over him. An Army retiree that loved his daughter very much. A warming yet intimidating thought.

Mr. Rylatt folded his arms, eyes narrowing. Quinton stood still while the man scanned him head to toe. He gave a sharp nod, and his mustache lifted with his smile. But was it an approving smile, or possibly an 'I'll kill you and hide the body smile?'

"Glad you're here," Mr. Rylatt said and extended a hand.

Guess he passed the first screening. Quinton relaxed his shoulders and shook Mr. Rylatt's hand-- a crushing, bone crunching experience, but Quinton held his own.

"This was my grandfather's cabin," Mr. Rylatt said. "He built it with his bare hands."

Quinton nodded. Carpentry was not a skill he possessed, but he remained in awe of those who did.

"My father got it when my grandfather passed. When my father passed, none of my brothers or sisters wanted it, so they sold their part to me."

"It's in great condition, sir. You only use it once a year?"

"Rent it out most of the year. Georgie takes care of the hospitality side of things. She says I'm not hospitable enough. Guess she's right."

Quinton nodded but didn't respond. Mrs. Rylatt had a point.

"We let family visit and such," he said. "But we make sure we get it for Christmastime, through the new year, and some times when Mrs. Rylatt and I need a little getaway." He winked.

"Gross, Dad," Maddox called over the banister. "Hey,

Quinton, we're bunking up here."

"Again, we're happy to have you here. Any friend of Maddox and Audria is a friend of ours." Mr. Rylatt gave him a quick pat.

"Thank you, sir."

"Would you help me and Maddox chop up more firewood later?"

"Yes, sir."

"Look at that, Georgie," Mr. Rylatt called over his shoulder toward the kitchen. "Boy's got some manners and not afraid of a little hard work."

"I noticed." Mrs. Rylatt smiled, elbows deep in grocery bags. Audria walked through the door from the kitchen, face blotchy. The room quieted, but no one pressed, only offered affirming nods and smiles. She'd been on the porch for a while, and Quinton thought it best to give her space.

"I'm okay, everyone," she said. "What's for supper?"

"We can talk about that after you help me put away groceries." Mrs. Rylatt pushed a bag in her direction, and Audria complied.

Quinton tried not to stare and settled on helping her unpack the groceries.

They worked in silence while Mrs. Rylatt hummed a fun rendition of "Angels We Have Heard on High". Small patters and clicks sounded. Perry, the funniest looking pug on the planet, ran the perimeter of the room. Guess he liked this place, too.

After emptying several brown bags and filling the counter top, the job was done.

Dozens of eggs. Milk. Flour. Sugar. Sprinkles. Morsels. Guess they were baking.

Steak. Pot roast. Ham. Potatoes. Wow. He would put on a few pounds eating like this.

He looked in Audria's direction, and she gave a smile.

"Thank you," Mrs. Rylatt said.

"Hey, Quinton, come check out the rest of the place," Maddox said upon entering the kitchen.

"There's more?" How could that be possible? Quinton walked past the couch where Mr. Rylatt made himself comfortable, football playing on the big screen with the sound low. Perry had made a home on Mr. Rylatt's plump stomach.

"Jacuzzi hot tub on the back porch." Maddox signaled a thumb over his shoulder. "You brought your swimming trunks, right?"

"I...I think so." Did he? Nope. He sighed.

"We've got to go to town later, so we'll pick some up."

"We've got to go to town?"

"Remember?" Maddox jutted out his jaw, eyes wide.

"Oh, um, that's right." The gifts. He still had to make a gift for Audria and her family. What was he going to make? If his dad could make a necklace for his mom then surely, he too could make something just as lovely. Quinton pressed his thumbnail between his lips and tapped against his front tooth. The taps clicked like Morse code.

Morse code. *That's it.*

He knew what he was making. For Audria at least.

"You guys still working on your Christmas gifts, huh?" Audria teased.

"No." Maddox poked her side. "And I bet you've been done with yours for weeks now."

"Not weeks." She rolled her eyes and turned her attention to Quinton. Would time always slow when she looked his way? "Quinton, there's also foosball and a pool table in the basement."

"We've got a sauna down there now, too. An infrared one," Mr. Rylatt said from the couch.

"This place is like a resort." Wow. His dad wasn't going to believe it.

"We think of the customers and try to stay competitive in the rental market." Mr. Rylatt propped half his body on the couch armrest, and Perry grunted.

"Jason likes to think of things to add to the cabin and say it's for the customers when in fact we all know better," Mrs. Rylatt said. Everyone laughed.

"So, what do all of you do first?" Quinton directed the question to no one in particular.

"Well," Audria said as she neared. Her eyes, a deep greenish blue, were easy to dive into. "The first night is the laziest, but the best. We usually bake something--cookies or even macarons. Then we'll play a board game and hang out in the hot tub."

He drank in her voice and memorized her expressions and features. The way she talked with a smile. The light dusting of freckles over the top her nose gave her a girlishness, but she stood before him very much a woman.

"Quinton?" She laughed. "You there?"

Huh? Oh. He shook his head. "Yes, and yes."

"So, which one do you want to do first?"

What had she asked? He blinked trying to remember. She waited.

"We're going to the store first," Maddox said. He yanked on Quinton's arm before he could object. "Be back in an hour."

"Maddox." Audria slugged her brother in the arm with a loud smack. Wow, she could pack a punch. "Maybe he doesn't want to go right now."

"It's all good." Quinton tossed a grin her way. "I do need to go. And, I'd like very much if you could show me how you make those macarons when we get back."

Her face flushed, and his heart fell for her even

more. "I'd like that very much."

Maddox guffawed. "Don't sign me up for that. I'll be in the Jacuzzi."

"Your mom and I will be in the sauna. Don't come knocking," Mr. Rylatt said, voice booming from the couch. Mrs. Rylatt giggled, and they all grimaced. Maddox visibly shook.

"Anyway," Audria said. She removed her coat and hung it close to the door. "See you guys when you get back. Maybe we can sit in the Jacuzzi when we're done with the macarons?"

"We?" Now it was his turn to blush.

"I meant...we...as in you and I, I mean--" She fell over her words, face as red as the coat she hung on the wall. "All of us can sit in it. Together."

"Now that's crystal clear, Sis."

"Go." She pointed to the door.

Quinton smiled and headed out, Maddox leading the way.

Making cookies with Audria was one thought, but sitting beside her in a Jacuzzi? Quinton palmed his forehead. *Oh, Lord.*

Chapter Fourteen

NIGHT SETTLED AROUND their cabin. A glow from the fireplace added to the ambiance, its warmth flooded into the kitchen. Audria stood at the counter sorting ingredients for their baking endeavor.

What a wonderful day. A full day. An emotional day, but good.

"Dinner was amazing." Quinton kept his distance, elbows on the counter.

"Mom makes a wonderful lasagna."

"Your family, they're great people."

"They are pretty wonderful, huh?"

"There seem to be so many traditions. Traditions you like doing together."

"Ha. Sometimes. The family picture seems to be a source of contention. Mom is bent on having it in front of the Christmas tree."

"And your dad?"

"His latest vote is for in front of the cabin, and Maddox doesn't really care. He's not able to always be home this time of year."

"Army life."

"Yeah." She kept the sigh to herself, pulled her hair into a quick side bun and washed her hands. Quinton washed his, too. His shoulder bumped against hers, and heat climbed her neck. The kitchen was hot enough.

"Ready for macaron lessons," he said.

"First thing to know--" Audria scooted the glass bowls apart. She reached for the whisk attachments for the mixer. "A perfect macaron is chewy on the inside and crunchy on the out, with a smooth top."

"Got it. Chewy on the inside. Crunchy on the out. Smooth top."

"We've had the egg whites sitting out, and that's important." She swung the whisk like a wand and attached it to the mixer. "They need to sit at room temperature for around thirty minutes or so."

"Why?"

"It makes a fluffier meringue. Here." Audria tossed Quinton an apron and grabbed one for herself. She tucked her head through the ribbon, but the straps to tie around her waist were knotted. Pulling made it worse.

"Let me help," Quinton said.

Before she could object, his hands were close, chest near her back. His breaths were slow, hands gentle. He pulled and tied. Audria worked to keep her thoughts on anything but him.

"All done."

"Thank you." If she turned now, they'd be too close. Their lips would be mere inches apart. She hadn't kissed anyone since Clay. Part of her wondered what it might be like to kiss another, to kiss Quinton, yet the other part fought to remain true and loyal to Clay.

Be open. The thought echoed in her mind. *I'm trying.*

Quinton must have sensed her unease because he moved to the side. For that, she was thankful, at least for now.

She cleared her throat. "We're going to add all the dry ingredients in a food processor, and then we'll sift it when done."

"It already looks chopped up to me."

His expression made her laugh. "Yes, but we want it to be even more fine."

"We do?"

"We do."

She blended and watched Quinton. He looked like he would take notes if he could.

"I am way in over my head here."

She pulsed the processor a few more times, and then began sifting. "It took me a while to get the hang of it. And I still bomb some batches."

"Have you always cooked?"

"Baked. Believe me, there's a difference. And my gran-mere taught me. She was from France, and her parents owned a bakery for decades before her."

"That's incredible."

"It is." Audria slid the dry ingredients aside and reached for another glass bowl and the sticks of butter. "I'd like to go to France one day and see if the building is still there."

"So, you're French. That's cool."

"And Irish, hence the hair. And I'm sure a host of other European ethnicities."

"I'm African American and bunch of those European ethnicities, too."

"I've always liked how diverse God made people. Different versions, kinds, and colors. He's pretty creative." Audria nodded. "Kind of like macarons. Same cookie, but all different kinds of flavors and colors."

"And what flavor of macaron are we making tonight?

"A traditional French Vanilla Bean." She attempted a French accent but failed. Quinton laughed, deep dimples forming in those cheeks, and the warmth in the kitchen returned. Goodness.

"Now, for the wet ingredients." She pointed to the bowl. "We'll used gel food coloring when it's time. It gives a more vibrant color."

"I didn't know there were different kinds of food coloring."

"So much to learn. Tsk. Tsk." She helped him separate the egg whites, added a pinch of salt, and began to whisk them until frothy. A little sugar added at a time until peaks formed. A bit of vanilla. Now a drop or two of red gel coloring and more whisking until the meringue was perfect.

"You're doing great," she said and soaked up Quinton's smile. "Now, let's macronage."

"What?"

"It's when we fold in the dry and wet ingredients."

"Oh, okay. Marconage away then."

In no time, they were piping the batter on to parchment paper.

Audria swiped her hands together and opened the oven door. "Three hundred degrees for seventeen minutes. We'll make vanilla buttercream for the filling. Nothing too fancy to start with."

"All of this is fancy."

Audria blended the butter, sifted in powdered sugar and the remaining ingredients. She filled a piping bag and placed it on the counter. "Now, we wait."

"Then?"

"We wait some more." She laughed and shrugged. "The cookie tops will need to sit for an hour before we fill them, and then we need to let them rest for twenty-four hours before we eat them."

"I don't know if that's gonna be possible."

"Tastes so much better, though. Totally worth the wait."

"I guess all good things are worth waiting for." His smile said so much.

Be open. Her face warmed, and she had to look away.

"I don't know if this is the right time, but I need to tell you something." Quinton untied his apron and placed it over a stool.

His expression caused her to worry. What could he possibly need to tell her?

Was he seeing someone else? Maybe he didn't feel for her what she was feeling for him. How stupid had she been to fall for someone she barely knew?

"Is there somewhere we could chat alone?" Quinton folded and unfolded his arms.

"The porch?" Fresh night air would probably help her thoughts and ease the pain of whatever Quinton was going to tell her.

Quinton held the door for her. Why did he have to be such a gentleman?

She kept her arms tight around her body, locking one hand onto an elbow. The door shut behind her, and then it was the two of them. Alone. The cool air swirled around them. Mom, Dad, and Maddox peeked out the side window, and Audria shooed them away. Was there no end to their meddling ways?

"We're not going to be eaten out here by a bear or anything, are we?" Quinton asked.

Audria giggled, thankful for the comic relief, and buried her chin in her sweater. "We might see a raccoon or two, but no bear. Not this time of year."

"That's a good thing. Don't really want to go down that way, you know?"

She laughed again, and the night settled between

them once more. The glow from the fireplace offered a subtle source of lighting through the cabin windows.

"Audria, I...I've really enjoyed getting to know you."

Here it came. She held tighter, one palm now clinging to her shoulder.

"Quinton." Her voice gave her a surprise. "I...I...I know we're still getting to know each other, but I know there's something between us."

"You do?" He seemed shocked and took a step forward.

"I guess it's obvious now that you must not feel the same way I feel about you, but I hope we can remain friends."

"Audria," he said and closed the remaining space between them. His face lowered and hovered over hers. She breathed him in, legs weakening. "I have feelings for you, too."

"Then...what...what are you going to tell me?"

"Audria, I need you to know that I care deeply for you. More than anyone before." He took her hands in his. She searched his eyes, wanting to know what could possibly bring him so much frustration at this moment. "But before we can move on, I need you to know that I knew Clay."

Clay. Her legs buckled for an instant. "You knew him?"

And he was just now telling her?

"We were friends."

The air left her lungs. All thoughts fled.

***

Audria wrapped one arm around her waist and clenched the porch railing.

It shouldn't feel like she'd been punched. This shouldn't have been a surprise at all, really. It only made sense if Maddox and Quinton were friends, then

Quinton would have at least known Clay. Did it make a difference now? Her thoughts spun.

The cabin. The memories. Maybe it was all too much for now. Maybe she'd been too open.

"Audria, I should have said something sooner. I truly didn't think about bringing it up."

"I believe you. I do." She did, but it still hurt. "It's just..."

If Clay had lived, so much would have been different.

Quinton laid his hand on top of hers, eyes sincere. "I'm sorry. I would never hurt you like that."

"You knew he and I were engaged?"

Quinton nodded, and her heart throbbed a bit more.

She let her mind wander through the memories, the real ones, and the ones imagined. A life she once dreamed with Clay. How many children they'd have. Holidays spent at the cabin. Life's adventures waiting.

"Clay was a good man. A Godly man." Quinton's eyes watered.

"Yes, he was." The thing she loved most about him was his passion for God and others. He lived his life on mission. Why God took him, she'd never understand this side of heaven. Even if God explained, she'd probably still not understand, nor would it quench the grief.

"I, um, I never shared this with anyone before," Quinton said. He tucked his chin and then lifted his face. "The night before Clay passed..." He pressed a fist to his lips, jaw tightening. A tear fell from his cheek, and she wiped it for him. "He, he's the reason I dedicated my life to Christ."

Her lips parted.

"Remember how I told you I made some bad choices as a teen and ended up on the streets?"

Audria managed a nod, her body shaking. Her heart

steadied. A peace spread throughout and stilled her jittering limbs.

"I was angry at God for taking my mom. I was mad at my dad for still loving a God who would do such a thing, and so I ran. I ran as far from God as possible." He turned for a moment, peering into the darkness. "Some kind strangers found me in an alley, helped me get straight." His smile was soft but pained. "It's where I got the idea for the station rotation event."

Audria held a hand over her heart. He had been on the receiving end of such kindness and paid it forward. "Quinton."

Her breath pressed passed her lips, but words to express the awe she felt wouldn't form.

"The Army gave me direction," he said. "Saved my life in many ways, but it was Clay's message of salvation that saved my soul."

She closed her eyes, letting the tears fall, and imagined the scene--one she could see well.

Quinton continued, "I was heading out on mission and stopped in to get some macarons."

"From one of the boxes I sent." Aduria wiped her cheeks with the back of her palm. "He loved those."

"He introduced me to them. I thought they were girly looking, and I made fun of him for eating them." He laughed, and his breath made puffs of smoke in the night. "They may be dainty and all, but I was hooked." His smile faded, and she felt hers falter as well. "I was in a rough relationship. We broke up that day on Christmas Eve. Clay listened, prayed with me, and pointed me back to God."

Audria squeezed his hand.

"The rest is history, really." He shrugged. "The next day, well, it was Christmas, and..."

They both fell quiet. Clay was killed by a roadside

bomb that struck his Humvee. The news came hours later while she sat by the Christmas tree waiting for a call from Clay that never came. That day had been a blur...

Clay's parents were the ones to call her. The cries. The sobs. Some memories never fade.

Quinton raked a hand over his head and rubbed the back of his neck. His striped pattern crew neck sweater bunched at the movement. "None of this makes sense, but God seems to work best that way. I don't know why Clay had to go, but I do know it was because of Clay that I know where I'm going when I die, and it was because of your macarons that I even went to talk to him in the first place that night." He shook his head as if trying to understand. "So, thank you, Clay, and thank you, Audria."

Audria pressed her fingertips over her mouth. A cry hitched in her throat. She'd spent years sending care packages to Clay and Maddox, not once thinking of the significance. God truly worked in mysterious ways.

"I don't know where we go from here--you and I," Quinton said. "I understand if you just want to remain friends."

They were already more than friends. Perhaps this was the first time she admitted it to herself.

Audria lowered her eyes and then stepped closer. "I'm scared, but I also can't deny what I feel for you."

"I'm scared, too." He brushed a lose strand of hair back from her face and smiled. "We'll take things as slow as you like."

"Thank you." She kept her voice a whisper. *Be open.* The words replayed in her mind and pried her heart open. Courage filled her. She rose onto the toes of her shoes and slid her hands to his shoulders until her wrists crossed behind his neck. Her heart pounded inside her chest. His scent, clean and masculine, drew her farther. She watched his pulse beat out a quick rhythm in his neck. He was nervous, too.

Quinton lowered his head, lips drawing near to hers. His hands folded into the small of her back, and he pulled her close with such care. No distance at all. His nose skimmed hers, and he paused, hovering as if asking permission. She replied with a tilt of her head, and his lips covered hers.

A tear fell, a joyous expression. The night grew colder, but waves of warmth washed over her. A soft chill touched her cheeks and dotted her lashes, leaving a damp mark in its place. She opened her eyes for a fluttering second. Snow.

It was snowing.

If rain brought renewal in the warmer months, surely snow brought it in the winter. A laugh worked its way from her mouth, and Quinton pulled away, eyes dazed. She laughed harder and held out her palm to the sky, embracing the revival. He wrapped an arm around her waist, and they watched the snow begin to fall in droves. It glistened in the light of the moon's blue hue. The scent of pine. The quiet.

All was well.

She turned to Quinton. Small snowflakes gathered on his shoulders, one landing on the tip of his nose. *Adorable.*

Audria dissolved the flake with the tip of her finger and kissed him again. If this was part of being open, it was one she could handle.

"Hey." The cabin door swung open. She and Quinton startled, but neither released their embrace. They stared at Maddox, whose grin grew larger than normal. He held up his phone, camera lens pointed in their direction. "I knew it."

"Go away, Maddox." Audria tried to scowl but surely failed miserably.

"Say 'hi' for Nora."

"Put it away." Audria arched a brow, her patience ending with him. "Are you even an adult?"

"That's debatable," Quinton said.

Maddox slid the phone into his back pocket. "Just keeping her in the loop, since you're not answering your calls or texts."

"I've been busy."

"I see that now."

Impossible. Audria huffed and would've stomped her foot if it would've helped.

"C'mon, Sis. Just trying to make you laugh a little." He grinned, and her frustration lessened. "Hitting the hot tub in a few and wanted to warn you that our little friend is out here."

"Little friend?" Quinton looked around and past Audria.

"Audria didn't mention Rocky?"

"Rocky?" Quinton looked to her.

"The raccoon," she said. "Perry the Pug. Rocky the Raccoon. Dad names them all."

"Oh." Quinton pursed his lips, face in a pinched expression. "Creative. So, Rocky's here?"

"Right there actually." Maddox pointed.

She and Quinton turned to find the creature lounging on the top step watching them. His fat belly protruded from his furry sides. The Christmas season suited Rocky well. Contents of trashcans from nearby cabins certainly held untold feasts for the greedy beast.

"Looks like Rocky got a good dinner and a show tonight." Maddox winked and turned. "See you guys in the hot tub."

Quinton looked from Maddox to her, his eyes wide. "Um, are we safe out here?"

"Just don't pet him," Audria said. "And, we have to

make sure to lock the doors. He can open them."

"What?"

Audria nearly doubled over laughing. "You're a soldier."

"I wasn't trained to fight a raccoon." Quinton stepped toward the door, a grin cracking on his face. "I didn't come all the way from Afghanistan to be taken out by an obese mammal."

Audria laughed harder, and an abrupt snort slipped out of her mouth. Heat flashed on her face.

Now Quinton doubled over. His laughter echoed in the night and sent Rocky on his way. "I'm learning so much about you."

"All the embarrassing stuff."

"All the stuff that makes me care even more about you."

Being open wasn't so bad. Not bad at all.

Chapter Fifteen

THE CHILL WAS a bit much. Audria clung to the robe wrapped around her body and shut the back porch door as quickly as possible. She tiptoe-hurried over to the hot tub and squeaked the whole way, as if the sound made the weather warmer.

"Move over," she said to Maddox.

He laughed, lifting his mug of hot chocolate in greeting. "Where's Quinton?"

"Calling his dad. He'll be down in a bit." She shivered and pranced while waiting for Maddox to scoot. "Hurry."

Maddox placed his mug on the porch railing then patted the edge of the hot tub. "Come on in."

"Gladly." She shed her robe and tossed it on a nearby rocking chair that sat like a butler holding several towels.

"Ick." Maddox scrunched his face. "What are you wearing?"

"What? It's vintage."

"It's hideous. Like something a grandma would wear."

"Whatever. I like it." And it was modest. Cute and

modest were hard to find these days.

Audria shrugged and sat on the side of the hot tub. The water bubbled and gurgled and smelled of sea salt and lavender. *So nice.* So inviting. She slipped in her feet.

"Ooh. Hot. Ouch." Audria seethed through her teeth, nearly losing her balance. Maddox chuckled while she gained composure, pulled her hair into a quick messy bun, and eased into the soothing waters.

"It's good to see you again, Sis." Maddox bobbed his head, long arms stretched along the back of the hot tub.

"You, too," she said and tossed him a smile. Though his face smiled, Audria could see the fatigue from travel and war. "You've got to be tired."

"I'll sleep late in the morning." He shrugged. "Just glad to be home. Don't want to miss anything."

She understood. Time spent with loved ones and unmentioned moments in life often turned to memories without ever being truly held or cherished. She, like Maddox, knew all too well the sanctity of a moment, of words both spoken and not. Audria spread her hands through the water and watched tiny bubbles dance along the edge of her fingertips.

The moonlight peeked from the evergreens, and soon the only sound was the humming and bubbling of the hot tub.

Audria didn't pry when talking with Maddox. She let him lead the conversation, never sure when her questions might touch a sore place in his heart. While he was still very much her older, protective, fun-loving brother, Maddox held hurts he never let her see. Perhaps that was part of being a soldier.

"What are you thinking about?" Maddox splashed water in her direction, and she grimaced. "Don't say 'nothing' either 'cause I know when you're lying."

Ah, yes, Maddox also had that whole lie-detector

ability going for him.

"I'm honestly not sure what I'm thinking. A bunch of jumbled stuff."

"If I had your brain, I'd be jumbled for sure."

She flicked water in his direction, and he cracked a smile.

Audria leaned back and rested her neck, letting her shoulders relax. She closed her eyes. "I'm thinking you always worry about others."

A long pause. Audria opened one eye to see him very much in deep thought.

He sighed. "I think that runs in our family."

She nodded. "Can we talk about why you invited Quinton?"

"Are you upset?"

"No, but--"

"Then, let's leave it at that. I'm looking out for my little sis and her best interest."

He seemed a bit testy, and Audria knew her words had stepped too close to some tender spot. She bent her legs, and draped one arm over a knee. Steam rolled in waves from the water and lifted into the night sky.

"Maddox?"

"Hmm?"

"You know I'm an adult now, right?"

He grinned and nodded.

"I'm capable of taking care of myself and making my own decisions."

He nodded a bit slower this time.

"I'd like to have a serious conversation. To really talk to you, and listen."

Maddox squirmed and fidgeted with this fingers steepling them just above the water.

Audria continued, "Please, just answer my questions without evading them or making a joke. You're my brother, I love you. I want to talk."

His jaw twinged and she swore she saw the glint of a tear forming in the corner of his eye. He cleared his throat. "I'm an open book."

"Why did you invite Quinton?"

"He's the right guy for you."

"Okay." Not that she had an argument, but... "Why have you worked so hard to plan all of this? Do you not trust my own judgment in picking a man?"

"Because..."

Audria waited, but Maddox only lowered his head. And then it hit her. "Clay."

She pressed her fingertips over her lips, the warm water seemingly turning colder. Maddox lifted his head, and the brokenness in his eyes tugged at her heart. He blamed himself for Clay. How had she not seen this?

"I'm so sorry, Audria."

"You are not at fault, Maddox."

"If I hadn't introduced the two of you--"

"Then I would never have had the opportunity to meet one of the greatest men to walk this Earth." She moved forward through the swirling waters. "I don't regret any of my time with Clay, nor do I blame you. I'm grateful, Maddox. Thank you."

He took in a hearty breath, eyes watering. "I thought helping you find someone else was a way to make up for..."

"There's nothing to make up for, or replace."

"You were crushed, Audria. Something died in you when Clay passed." He cupped a hand over his chin for a moment and then let it fall. "My job was always to protect you, and I had--"

"Had done nothing wrong. It's no one's fault."

He sighed and locked his palms behind his head. "He was a great friend. The best."

Audria tucked her chin. She'd spent nearly two years blaming herself, never once considering how Maddox felt. Grief has the ability to blind.

Maddox pulled himself from the water and sat on the edge of the hot tub, feet submerged. He shook his head. "Do you remember falling from the tree house?"

Audria made a face. "Why are you changing the topic?"

They were finally having a real conversation.

"Just answer," he said through a huff.

"Yes, why?"

"You fell because of me."

"What? No, I was about to climb down, when..." When? She couldn't remember. Her five-year old version of the event was simply falling and waking up in the Emergency Room.

"You were always following me around, and my friends and I were trying to hide from you. I yelled at you to leave, and when you turned to go--" Maddox looked away. "I thought it would be funny to trip you, but it wasn't."

Audria rubbed at the faint scar above her brow. She hadn't thought of the injury in years, nor did it matter now.

"Maddox, you were ten, and we were kids. I remember how annoying I was."

"I thought I killed you."

"And so, you've spent the rest of your life trying to somehow make up for it?"

"Not make up for it, but to be better, to help and protect and take care of you and those I love."

His heart was as wide as it was deep. Audria grinned.

"Maddox, you're the best brother any girl could have. Please know I love you, and I don't harbor any unforgiveness toward you."

His smile grew, and he lunged forward, yanking her up into a choking hug.

Audria laughed. "But seriously, if you don't stop trying to fix me and hook me up with people, we're going to have issues."

He slipped back into the water and shrugged with one shoulder. "Not trying to hook you up with just anybody. You'll find Quinton to be on point. I've even had him background checked."

"Creepy, in a caring sort of way."

"So, what do you think about him?"

She smiled but didn't answer.

Maddox folded his arms across his chest with a smug grin. "That's what I thought."

"Shut up, you know-it-all," but her tone was far from angry.

***

Small clicks sounded on the porch, and Perry threw a fit inside the cabin. She and Maddox sat in the hot tub and through the glass doors watched the chubby pug run the length of the room.

"Sounds like Rocky's back," Maddox said. "Guess he really enjoyed that dinner and show tonight with you and Quinton on the porch."

He winked, and Audria slugged his shoulder. She shook her head and laughed.

Maddox continued, "And here comes Quinton. Looks like that's my cue to leave."

"What? No." Audria yanked on his arm as he attempted to leave. "It's inappropriate for he and I to be out here alone."

"There are glass doors. We see all. Besides, Rocky will stand guard."

Nice. She frowned but let him step away.

Quinton opened the door, towel thrown over one

shoulder and phone in his hand. Audria swallowed and attempted not to stare. *Oh, goodness.*

A godly man, with a body like that? Ugh. Audria hid her face for a moment to clear her head.

"Y'all have fun." Maddox smacked Quinton on the shoulder. "Don't sit too close to her."

Quinton nodded quickly. "You leaving? Now?"

The man appeared scared. A funny thought.

"She's talked my ear off, and all I wanted to do was get some sleep."

"Hey!" Audria tossed a handful of water at Maddox but missed. It landed at Quinton's feet with a small splash. She shrugged an apology.

The door closed, which left the two of them, well three. Rocky sat near the corner of the porch staring back at them.

Quinton backed away from the beast and took a sit on the edge of the hot tub. "Is that thing going to be an issue?"

"Shouldn't be."

"What's he doing?" Quinton's face folded into a disgusted grimace.

"He and Perry have this love/hate relationship thing going."

The raccoon paced along the windowsill, back arched, hair raised, and Perry threw an absolute barking fit inside. Mom and Dad both yelled at him from their seat on the couch, but Perry would not relent.

"You sure Perry's not going to stroke out or something?"

Audria laughed. "They'll settle down in a bit, and then they just stare."

"Stare?"

"Yeah," she said through a giggle. "They have this hour-long staring contest until Mom or Dad shoos them both away with a broom."

"Wow."

"Then they'll go at it again tomorrow night."

"Weird." Quinton chuckled as he eased into the water. "Your family has some of the funniest traditions."

"You don't know the half." She nodded and sat back. "What about your family? How's your dad?"

Quinton placed his phone on the porch railing, the screen still glowing. "He's doing really well and excited to meet you."

Meet me? Audria tried to hide her gulp. What had he told his father about her that would make him want to meet her? The thoughts filled her head.

"Said they're in a small village right now feeding the people and giving medical care."

"It has to be hard being away from him this time of year."

Quinton nodded, folding and unfolding his arms, appearing very uncomfortable. That made two of them. Sitting here, alone, in a hot tub, with someone so gorgeous, next to a raccoon and a barking pug. Ha. Hilarious. Audria laughed out loud, and Quinton joined her.

"This is all a bit funny, huh?"

She squinted and pinched her thumb and index finger close together. "Just a little bit."

"So, yes, it is hard being away from Dad, but it's kind of been our life for a long time. His ministry as a pastor overseas takes him away just as much as I'm away."

"Was he always a pastor?"

Quinton nodded. "Since before I was born. He served in the Army as a medic for a while before getting out and becoming a pastor. He met Mom while on a mission trip. Would you like to see a picture of her?" His eyes lit up.

"Very much."

Quinton dried his hands on a nearby towel and reached for his phone. "Dad texted me several pics that I hadn't seen in years. He thought you might like to see them, too."

Her heart quickened. Not only did Quinton seem intent on her meeting his father, but his father also wanted her to meet Quinton's mother. What had he and his father talked about? Her heart raced faster. Quinton indeed must have deep feelings for her. Were hers as deep? She swallowed back the dryness in her throat.

"Here's this one." Quinton moved close enough to make her face warm. She dried her hands off and held the phone, gazing at the beautiful couple on the screen.

The woman's eyes were shaped like Quinton's, and her smile was similar. Her skin was deep and warm, the color of milk chocolate. She nestled beneath the arm of a towering, young, broad-shouldered man whose skin was nearly as pale as Audria's.

"They're beautiful." Captured in this moment, forever smiling, forever in love. "What was her name?"

"Serenity," he said in a near whisper. "She was as serene and peaceful as her name implied."

"And your dad's name?"

"Aidan."

Serenity and Aidan.

"Dad has never remarried and says he never will."

A part of Audria understood his father's feelings. She drew in a breath and stared at the woman on the screen-- the mother to such an incredible man, who left this world too soon. If by some chance she could see down from above, somehow peer into this moment, Audria prayed Serenity could see how amazing Quinton was.

What would it have been like to have met her? To sit with both Quinton's mother and father, perhaps over a meal, or perhaps a family outing? She let her mind wonder and imagine for a moment a life built alongside Quinton. Her heart pounded in her chest, and Audria forced her imagination to settle.

"This picture was taken the day Dad proposed." Quinton's voice carried so much pride. "It caused a bit of a stir in both of their families."

"'Cause of their skin color?"

He nodded. "But they all came around." Quinton chuckled. "My Gramps-- Mom's father, called Dad 'Viking man.' He'd say, 'why'd you have to go off and marry a Viking?'"

Audria laughed. "Your dad does have that appearance." Guess that's where Quinton got his build. Her eyes fell to his shoulders and chest for a mere instant before she drew her focus back to the screen.

Quinton swiped, and a new photo appeared. Serenity sat on a porch swing swaddling an infant. Quinton stared, and the night grew silent. Perry and Rocky had begun their staring contest. He eyed them and smiled then scooted a bit closer to Audria, but she didn't mind in the least.

"This was the day they brought me home from the hospital," he said.

"You're precious."

"I apparently had the largest head the doctor had ever seen."

She giggled, and he swiped the screen again and again pausing at each one to commentate. Quinton's life scrolled before her in one amazing sequence. Serenity holding a birthday cake. Christmas presents, smiles, first days of school, bumps, bruises, she was there for it all.

"And this is the last picture I took with her." Quinton's tone grew solemn. Audria rested her cheek on his shoulder and peered down at the picture. Serenity had grown frail, her body thinning, but her smile as bold and bright as ever. A twelve-year-old Quinton sat at her side on a floral couch, his hand in hers.

Audria bit down on her bottom lip to keep tears from forming, but they came regardless. She sniffled and dabbed at the corner of her eyes.

"She died on New Year's Day," he said. "We sang her favorite hymns while she slipped into heaven."

Tears fell down her cheeks. The holidays were hard on Quinton, too, yet he looked at them with such hope.

He clicked the screen, and Serenity's light faded. Quinton slid the phone back onto the porch railing.

"Thank you for sharing these memories with me," Audria said.

He nodded. "It took me a long time to embrace hope after losing Mom, and it took me just as long to enjoy the Christmas season again."

He reached for her hand and they intertwined fingers, now sitting side by side. "Part of me completely understands why it's been so hard for you."

She nodded and sniffed once more. He pressed a finger to her cheek to wipe away the last tear trailing down her face. "I'm glad I came here."

"Me, too."

They turned, faces close, lips drawing closer. He hovered and then pulled away, clearing his throat.

"Is everything okay?" She sat up eyes fluttering.

"They're staring at us."

"Huh? Who?" Audria turned her neck until it ached. "Oh. Them."

Perry and Rocky.

"Forget them," she said through a laugh and kissed him.

Chapter Sixteen

IT WAS JUST past noon when Quinton finally woke. Maddox pegged him with a folded sock. Not the best way to wake up, but effective.

"Let's get ready to go tubing," Maddox said.

Quinton stretched and yawned, working to shed the jet lag away. Time change was the worst part of traveling.

"How long has everyone else been up?" Quinton sat, pillow tucked under his elbow. He yawned again and swiped a hand over his face.

"You mean, how long has Tooter been up?"

Quinton frowned, but shrugged. "I hate sleeping past everyone."

"They get it. Trust me. And she actually woke up not long ago. Guess she had a really late night."

"Hmm." Yes, before they had realized it, it had been three in the morning. Quinton had forced himself to bid her goodnight. He stretched out his hands, remembering holding hers. What an incredible evening talking in the hot tub. And that kiss...

"How in the world are the two of you able to talk so

much? Don't you run out of things to say?"

He thought, head tilted until his neck strained a bit. "I could talk to her forever."

"Wow. Just wow. Do you even know how sappy that sounds?"

"Hey, you're the one who introduced us." Quinton grinned and scooted from the bottom bunk.

"I know a good match when I see one." Maddox tugged on a snow suit and zipped it to his chest. "Mom has some biscuits and country ham waiting. We can grab one on our way out."

Wow. This place. This family. Hospitality was like their middle name or something. Quinton stood and stretched high and then low. "What about you?"

"I'll probably have two biscuits."

"Nah, man, what about a match for you?"

Maddox paused, and Quinton arched his back, twisting side to side.

"I ain't got time for all that."

"And I do?"

"Dad wants us to bring in some more wood."

"Nice topic change. I see what you did there."

Maddox grinned and pulled gloves from his pocket. "Don't worry about me. My time will come."

Quinton nodded and reached for his snow suit hanging over the end of the bed. "Well, thank you."

"Don't get all mushy on me."

"I'm serious man, thank you."

"Don't thank me too soon."

"Really, your family and Audria, it's like, it's like a dream coming true that I never would have dared to dream or thought to dream of." He fluffed his pillow and made the bed, smoothing out the creases in the blanket with a wide swipe of his hand.

"You've heard her snort, right? And you know why

she has the nickname Tooter?"

Quinton grinned.

"And you're still sticking around?"

Quinton laughed and knelt to slip on a fresh pair of socks.

"Come on," Maddox said. "Let's get this day going."

"Can't wait." Quinton zipped up his suit and followed behind Maddox, sending a prayer for Maddox to one day find a match, to know the kind of love that Quinton felt for Audria.

***

Quinton wiped his hands. That should be plenty of firewood. He worked alongside Maddox stacking the ricks of wood against the shed and then hauling heaping armfuls inside. Snow crunched beneath his boots. He climbed the steps of the back deck and stomped the excess snow from his soles before entering the cabin with a quiet grunt.

"How long will this last us?" he asked Maddox.

"Three or four days."

"I was thinking maybe a century."

Maddox chuckled. "This should be enough for inside. For now, at least."

Quinton laid the logs in a neat row, triple stacked by the fireplace. He warmed his hands in front of the fire and blew warm air into his palms.

"Good work, fellas." Mr. Rylatt came in from the cold and closed the cabin door. Mr. Rylatt held his own out there, splitting logs and hauling them up the steps. No break or pause either. The man kept at it, even when Quinton prayed he'd relent. What a work out.

"Dad, no more firewood today. You're killing us." Maddox arched his back, near out of breath.

"You young bucks still got a lot of miles on ya." Mr. Rylatt laughed and knelt to pet Perry. The pug lapped up the attention.

Perry paused in front of Quinton, eyes big and bugged. What did he want?

He wasn't opposed to animals. Quite liked them really, minus nosey, obese raccoons. A pet wasn't something he had much time for in the Army, though. Maybe one day.

"He wants you to pet him," Mr. Rylatt said.

Maddox smirked. "Consider yourself lucky enough to get this close to Perry."

Quinton nodded, palms suddenly growing damp. All these nerves over a pug? Perry licked his nose, his stare growing intense. "Sure he won't bite?"

"Nothing's ever a hundred percent." Mr. Rylatt gave Quinton a solid smack on the back. "Tooter, Georgie, we're ready to tube."

"Coming," Audria called from upstairs somewhere.

Mrs. Rylatt peeked her head from the kitchen. "If you want more homemade hot chocolate then you'll wait, sweetheart."

Her tone was a mix of sweet and stern, and Mr. Rylatt nodded like a soldier taking orders.

"Perry's still waiting," Maddox said, grin growing.

And he was. Perry stared, one tooth now snaggled out front. And he made this grunting sound. Was that normal?

So far, Quinton had met Mr. Rylatt's approval, so why in the world did it matter what Perry thought of him? What was next? The approval of Rocky the Raccoon? Quinton laughed to himself. *I'm being ridiculous.*

He knelt and offered a hand for Perry to sniff in greeting, since a handshake wouldn't do. The pug's eyes widened; his wet nose searched Quinton's palm and the back of his knuckles. Should he have brought a snack?

Perry paused, turned his head from Mr. Rylatt, then

slowly to Maddox. And then, the unexpected. The dog nodded. No kidding. He nodded.

"Looks like he's cool with you," Maddox said with a shrug.

"He seriously nodded?" Quinton rocked back on his heels, disbelief surely covering his face.

"Go ahead and pet him before he changes his mind," Mr. Rylatt said and shuffled to the kitchen. "Dogs are a great judge of character," he called over his shoulder.

Glad Quinton's character passed, but for a dog to sit as the judge? Strange, yet somehow Perry's acceptance made life a bit more pleasant. Quinton petted him between the shoulder blades, working his fingers through the furry rolls and wrinkles in a small circular motion.

"I'm ready," Audria said. She leaned over the balcony, smile wide, and Quinton's heart raced. He waved and watched her hurry down the stairs while Perry vied for more attention. Quinton scooted him away with considerable effort and greeted Audria with a quick hug that caused Maddox to arch a brow.

"Let's go," she said and practically dragged him out the door.

"I don't know what I'm doing."

"It'll be fun," she said.

"So, typically when I hear 'it'll be fun,' someone ends up in the hospital."

Maddox nearly doubled over laughing. "Soldiers have the best kinds of those stories."

So very true.

In no time at all, he and the Rylatt family were outside, bundled in snow suits and lugging enormous snow tubes up the hill behind the cabin.

Quinton stared down the hillside, noting the barrage of spindly trees at the bottom.

"Where's that skydiving-adrenaline-junky spirit?" she

teased, poking an elbow into his side.

Quinton puffed his cheeks. The woman had a point. "Just don't want to hurt myself in front of you."

Or in front of her family.

She laughed. "It's the snowball fights that result in injuries. Tubing? You'll be fine."

He sighed. "Let's do this."

***

Night fell, and though he'd give anything for another evening of talking until three in the morning or later, Quinton knew he needed the rest. And so did she.

He climbed the steps and made his way to his cabin room, mind slipping on their moments shared.

What an incredible day. The snow, the tubing, her laughter...

His mind slipped into another memory and how the feel of her kiss remained on his lips. She must've felt it--that rushing warmth. The porch, the hot tub. *Good, Lord.*

The way she melted into his arms, he'd never forget. Ever.

Quinton sat and bent over the small wooden desk in the room he shared with Maddox in the cabin. Maddox slept on the top bunk, snoring, but Quinton paid no mind. He sorted out the items purchased at the store he and Maddox went to yesterday before the time he spent baking with Audria in the kitchen and then on the porch. He'd been honest with her--transparent to the core. She hadn't run. She listened, and then...that kiss. And then another kiss. Would he ever stop thinking of it? He prayed not.

She smelt of honey and cinnamon, and tasted of the same.

Focus, man.

Less than two days until Christmas. Crunch time. These gifts weren't going to make themselves, but his eyelids grew heavy. Life had been nonstop since he stepped off the plane stateside. Not complaining, but the constant yawning meant another morning of sleeping in would be necessary.

Quinton eyed the items. Wooden rounds, no more than four inches in diameter, ribbon, beads, wire, paint, a blank canvas, a hammer, and some kind of engraving and wood burning kit. Geez. *Where to begin?*

For the uncrafty, DIY wasn't something one did with certainty. In fact, the task reminded him of his mud-pie making days as a young boy. His mom always took them, smiling, and cooing over how beautiful they were. Quinton arched a brow. A mother's love had blinded her to his lack of crafting abilities, but perhaps Audria and her family would receive his attempt in the same manner.

He pushed the small engraving tool to the side and stifled a yawn. A bit longer, then sleep. He eyed the small tool, turning it over in his hands. Couldn't be too hard to use. Maybe watching a few YouTube DIY tutorials might be wise. The wire and pliers seemed a better place to start. Quinton cut three pieces of the rose gold wire. Two and a half inches would do just fine for what he needed.

Where were those beads? And the clasps? He shuffled a few items around until spotting them and continued working. Quinton counted out the beads, and recounted once more. He worked, his large fingers struggling to slide the beads in place--a frustrating experience. One by one, the beads slipped into place on the wire. Some fell and bounced on top of the desk. They rolled around for a few seconds before he could wrangle the speedy little things back between his pinched fingers. Crafting was not made for the uncrafty, or for those with large hands.

With the beads finally in their place, Quinton reached

for the pliers and bent each wire end into a tiny loop. *Not bad.*

If homemade gifts were meant to have meaning, then he wanted to get this right.

He continued working on Audria's gift, but his thoughts traveled back to that kiss then morphed into more recent moments from the day.

She held his hand earlier while racing up the hill behind the cabin. He'd never been snow tubing before, but it was more fun than he'd had in years. He shook his head as he recalled how the day had played out. She laughed, mouth wide, head back, hair flying beneath her knit hat and smacking him in the face as they slid down the snow together. They fell, the tube toppling over them, but Audria had not cared.

The woman was an adventure. Someone he could travel life with.

Quinton smiled. Was it possible to love someone within a month of knowing them? To want to spend the rest of his life with her?

With God, all things were possible.

Chapter Seventeen

IT WAS CHRISTMAS Eve, and Audria lay across her bed toying with the end of the pillow beneath her head. Sunlight peeked through the blinds. She squinted and rolled to her side.

Was Quinton awake?

And why was he her first thought? Audria ran a hand through her tangled hair and sat up, back pressed against the headboard. She leaned over and pulled her journal from the nightstand and thumbed through the pages.

Memories, moments, prayers, and praises all recorded.

Audria paused on an older entry. Two years ago, on Christmas Eve. Eerie how the post resembled today. At the cabin, cuddled in her bed, waking to the morning light, but on this day two years ago, her thoughts were of Clay. She cut the memory short and skimmed forward. Christmas Eve from last year. A heavier entry. The ink on the pages were blurred and spotted from her tears. Audria's eyes watered as she read her past plea to God. A plea for healing, hope, and direction.

God had answered those requests. Although, it wasn't an instant answer. Healing, hope, and direction came in a process. One she wasn't sure would ever end.

She turned the pages, and the dates played like a song. A symphony with high and low notes creating a melodious praise to God for working all things for her good.

A recent post caught her eye. Dated right after Thanksgiving. A simple prayer. *"Help me move on."*

Had she moved on? Perhaps not moved, but moving-- a continuous motion of growth.

Her phone buzzed, and Audria slid the screen to answer the call.

"Girl," Nora said, voice filled with obvious frustration. "Why am I getting all the juicy details from Maddox?"

"Juicy?" Audria laughed and gathered her knees to her chest.

"You kissed Quinton, and you sat in the Jacuzzi together--"

"Um, there are glass doors, so it wasn't like were totally alone--"

"Whatever. You went snow tubing together yesterday, and--"

"This is borderline stalking. I'm worried."

"How was the kiss? I need details. And hurry up 'cause the kids will be awake in like five minutes."

"The kiss..." Audria sighed and fell into the decorative pillows sprawled on top the bed. "It was...incredible. Magical."

She pressed a palm to her forehead, remembering the feel, the moment, the scent of the night air, and how the snow glistened. How tight he had held her.

"So, what do you think?"

"About the kiss? I just told you--"

"No, about him. Quinton. Do you think he could be--"

"I'm not ready to say that, but I like him a lot."

"A whole lot or just a lot?"

"Nora, I never thought I would feel this way about someone after Clay. I don't know what it means, but I want to find out."

Nora squealed, and Audria yanked the phone away from her ear. "Nora, shhh. Your kids are sleeping, remember."

"Oops," Nora said through a laugh. "So, what do you two love birds have planned for today?"

"It's all of us, not just he and I."

"Uh huh."

"We're going down to Gatlinburg today. See some of the sights, have a nice dinner, enjoy the lights, and Mom wants to go to the candlelight service at the chapel."

"I'm playing all of this out in my head, and it makes the best movie."

"I'm glad I can provide such entertainment for you."

"I hear one of the kids." Her voice lowered. Like that would help. "Before I go, I wanted to tell you Jayce's mom called me."

"Called you?"

"I am her son's principal." Nora clicked her tongue, and Audria laughed. "She was going to call you, too, but I told her you were living it up in the mountains."

"Is she okay? Jayce all right?"

"Girl, she's doing wonderful. Said because of the rotation event, she's been able to find quality childcare for her baby, and they have Internet now, which means Jayce has no reason not to do his homework when we get back, and she's enrolling in an online school."

Audria's heart stuck in her throat. She rolled from the bed and planted her feet on the cabin floorboards with a solid thud. "Nora, thank you for letting me know."

"And get this--"

"There's more?"

"One of the colleges that came to our event is offering her a scholarship."

Audria gasped, her legs working into an excited dance. Her crazy locks bounced around her shoulders. "What? I can't believe this."

"I know. Girl, it's a Christmas miracle. God is so good."

"Yes, He is." Audria spun, one hand raised to the ceiling.

"One more thing, and then I for real have to go." Nora's kids now chattered in the background, one demanding breakfast. She shushed them before continuing. "Check your email."

"Um, okay." Audria made a face, her hand falling to her side. "Should I be worried?"

"Just check your email, oh, and last thing...I need details on your date tonight."

"It's not a date."

"That's what you think."

"Nora, it's not a--"

"Bye." The phone went silent.

A date wouldn't be a bad thing. She tossed the idea around and let it go...for now.

After all, she and Quinton had shared a kiss. A kiss before the first date. Yikes, ugh. That didn't sound good...

Her phone buzzed. A text from Nora reminding her to check her email.

Fine. Audria smiled and checked her email from her phone.

A message from Jayce. *Oh, wow.*

Audria sat at the edge of the bed and let his sweet

message sink into her soul.

Dear Ms. Rylatt,

I don't remember you from school, guess you're not a teacher, but you're still important. You helped my mom and brother and I will forever thank you for that. I love them very much and I was trying to help them out all by myself because I'm the man of the house right now, but it was hard, and I started making some pretty bad choices. I'm not making bad choices now. Because of you I have hope that my future is going to be awesome, that my little brother's future will be awesome, and so will my mom's. Thank you. Merry Christmas.

-Jayce

She cried. Cried and smiled. Smiled and then cried more. In her effort to move on, she'd helped others move on as well. What a curious and wonderful thought. Audria held the phone to her chest and wondered what moving on would look like with regards to Quinton.

***

The streets of Gatlinburg buzzed with life and Christmas cheer. Beautiful lighted archways reached across the roads. Garland and wreaths adorned store windows, doors, and streetlights. Gatlinburg was made for Christmas--icy sidewalks and all.

Mom and Dad walked ahead, Maddox moseyed somewhere in the middle. Audria followed behind, Quinton at her side.

"This place really is something," Quinton said. He zipped his peacoat and buried his hands in the coat pockets. "And that steak. Wow."

"Peddler's is Dad's favorite steakhouse. We come every time we're here. They know him by name now, and send him home with scraps for Perry."

"That is one spoiled dog." Quinton's laugh was contagious.

"Wait 'til you see what Mom bought him."

"I'm surprised she didn't hand-make him a gift."

"I wouldn't put it past her."

Mom, Dad, and Maddox were several feet away now. Her family stared back over their shoulders with plotting smiles.

"I think they're trying to lose us on purpose," he said.

"Their scheming knows no end."

She and Quinton continued their stroll past pastry shops, arcades, families taking selfies.

"Wanna take a selfie with me?"

Audria giggled and shrugged. "Why not?"

Quinton slid his phone from his pocket and held it up. They leaned, heads touching, and smiled.

"How about another?" He pulled her closer, cheeks now together.

His stubble tickled her, and she turned, but her lips skimmed his just as he took the picture.

Audria pulled away. "I'm sorry."

"I'm not."

They stared at one another. A ring of air billowed past her lips and into the crowds pushing their way past. Audria steadied her legs and held to a lamppost covered with spiraling garland and lights. The twinkling small globes shone brighter as the sun took a bow. Christmas carols and merry chatter spilled from the doorways of mom and pop shops.

"We should probably move." Did she really just say that? Audria squinted, regretting her suggestion. Let the people pass, who cared?

He simply nodded and they continued on their way.

"Look," she said and pointed at the store window. Her favorite candy store. "They're pulling taffy."

Red and white stripes stretched and then folded in a cyclical, ongoing rotation.

"That's really neat." Quinton moved closer to the window, eyes wide. His genuine fascination gave him a boyish air. "They really make taffy like that?"

She nodded. "We can go in. They'll even let you sample fresh taffy."

"Really?"

"And you can sample the fudge."

"Sold." He made his way to the entrance in two strides. Audria hurried behind, careful not to slip.

Five samples later, Audria was tugging Quinton out the door. "You're going to be sick."

"It's so worth it."

"You might be right."

They continued forward taking turns pointing out lights, funny vintage signs, and perfect spots for quick selfies.

"I've always loved coming here." They paused on a bridge and watched the white river water rush below. She rubbed her hands together, wishing she brought her gloves. "Something about this place. I don't know. It's like how I imagine parts of heaven might be. Bright and cheerful. Smelling like candy." She laughed at her own silliness.

He smiled, those dimples forming, and her face warmed.

"Let's hope heaven's a bit warmer," he said and grinned. "Or that we'll have someone's hand to hold to help keep us warm."

The heat intensified between them, and she lowered her face. Quinton's hand waited like an open invitation. Audria drew in the late evening air and slid her hand into his. *Be open. Help me move on.*

Their fingers intertwined.

"Audria," he said, face drawing close to hers. "I love you."

The words struck. Her lips parted. Did she love him?

"Audria? Is that you?" a familiar voice called. She turned and met the faces of a not so distant past.

Clay? Her heart hammered. No, Clay was gone. The couple standing in front of her were older.

"Mr. and Mrs. Smith?" Clay's parents. Oh, how Mr. Smith resembled Clay. Her heart wrenched. Audria's hand fell from Quinton's, and she gripped the railing.

In an instant, the couple had wrapped their arms around her and kissed her cheek.

"Look at you," Mr. Smith said. He smiled wide, but a sadness remained in his eyes. A sadness, a void caused from losing their one and only child. "Haven't changed a bit. Still as pretty as a picture."

Mrs. Smith dotted her eyes. "Sam and I were just talking about you. What are the odds we'd run into you here?"

"Clay loved this place," said Mr. Smith. "Figured we'd spend some time here."

Her knees shook. Audria wasn't sure if her body or heart would make it tonight.

"How are you?" Mrs. Smith looped her arm in her husband's, nothing but kindness in her expression.

How am I? Audria wondered the same.

"I...I've...I'm doing well." Until now.

Quinton cleared his throat, and Audria startled. She'd forgotten he was only inches from her.

"And who is this?" Mrs. Smith gestured to Quinton, and Audria's mind went blank.

Who was he to her now? She blinked, no answer coming.

"I'm Captain Quinton Nolan," he said and extended his hand to them both. "I'm assuming you are--"

"Clay's parents," they said in unison with an affirming nod.

"He was a good man. I owe a lot to him. I'm so sorry for your loss," Quinton said.

"Thank you. You knew him?" Mrs. Smith stepped forward, eyes searching.

"Yes, ma'am," Quinton said.

"You look familiar." Mrs. Smith squinted. "Doesn't he, honey?"

Mr. Smith nodded. "Yes, he does."

They continued their conversation, Quinton shaking their hands and sharing his memories of Clay.

It pained Audria. Her throat tightened, and tears welled in her eyes until the Christmas lights blurred. She listened to Clay's parents talk about their son with Quinton. Listened and watched until her heart could bear no more.

"I'm so sorry. I have to go." Audria bit her lip to keep it from trembling and spun on the heels of her boots.

"Audria," Mrs. Smith called after her, but Audria kept her legs moving.

Quinton's voice sounded through the crowd, but Audria pushed past, not looking back. She quickened her pace. Deep sobs tore through her chest.

Why? Why did it still have to hurt?

She ducked behind a doorway and swiped at her eyes. *I can't do this. I can't be open. I can't move on.*

Maybe seeing Clay's parents was some sort of sign from God. Audria cradled her forehead in the palms of her hands trying to make sense of it all.

A few people stopped, and Audria felt their stares. She stepped from behind the doorway, and walked with her head down, arms across her body, holding herself together. She walked until her feet ached, until her face tingled from the cold, until the sound of a choir gave her reason to pause.

She lifted her eyes and watched as people flowed past and through the red doors of the little white chapel. An elderly man cradled a basket in the crook of his elbow and passed out candles to those entering. The Christmas Eve Candlelight Service. The man spotted her and held a candle in her direction, but her feet were anchored to the spot.

Chapter Eighteen

"AUDRIA." QUINTON CALLED her name, but she didn't slow, and soon he'd lost sight of her. The Smiths were incredibly apologetic, but there was no need for their apology. No one was at fault.

Quinton left the couple on the bridge, both holding on to each other. How had this magical evening turned so tragic?

Seeing Clay's parents must have been too much for her. And he had confessed his love only seconds before they arrived. Quinton groaned and picked up his pace. His soul ached for Audria and the confusion she must be feeling. He darted across the street and further down the sidewalk, lungs inhaling and exhaling the cold air.

He paused. The red coat in the distance caught his eye. *Audria.*

Quinton kept his distance.

She stood facing the small chapel as if contemplating entering. Folks passed her by, but she kept still.

Should he go to her?

The surrounding chill didn't bother him. He lifted his

chin and walked. Soft cries pierced his heart as he neared her.

"Audria." He touched her shoulder, but she didn't turn.

"Please, leave me be right now," she said through a small cry.

Quinton faced her, vying for eye contact, but she kept her head lowered.

"I'm here to listen."

"I don't know what to say."

He figured as much. Sometimes just being present was all that was needed.

They stood, the night air cool around them.

"Can we go in?" she asked, eyes focused on the little cottage-looking church.

"If you'd like."

She nodded, and they walked in silence.

The door-greeter handed each of them a candle as they walked through the arched double doors. Soft music played, and the glow of the sanctuary offered the peace and warmth his shaking soul desired. Quinton spotted Maddox and his parents sitting toward the front. If he could get their attention somehow without disrupting the service.

Maybe she would want to sit with them. Quinton gestured toward her family, but Audria shook her head and paused at the back pew. She sat, knees together, and cradled the candle between her palms. Tears streaked down her face.

Should he sit? Quinton debated, weighing the pros and cons, before sitting beside her careful to leave space.

The service began, and an elderly man in front of him turned to offer to light Quinton's candle with his own. Quinton nodded his thanks, and lent his candle to Audria. She sniffled and tilted the wick of her candle toward the flame. He watched the flame transfer, wishing very much he could transfer the hurt from her heart to his, to spread the peace and joy from his mind to hers.

Audria sniffled again. The way she cried, the way she wouldn't look at him--it all said goodbye in so many ways. Quinton closed his eyes to pray. It can't be over. It couldn't be. Quinton pushed his own selfish thoughts and requests aside and focused on Audria. *Lord, help her heal, right now, even if it means I'm not in the picture.*

***

The car ride home was silent. Quinton sat in the back seat, Maddox in the middle, and Audria miles apart on the other side. She gazed out the window, and Quinton wondered what she saw, or what she was thinking. Maybe he didn't want to know.

More than once, Quinton attempted small talk, but it quickly dissipated. Not even Maddox had anything to say. Mr. Rylatt drove, both hands on the wheel, jaw tight, and Mrs. Rylatt sat in the passenger seat, one hand cupping her chin. Quinton considered attempting to talk once more, but decided to stare out the window instead. Maybe he'd see what Audria saw.

Mountain roads were dark; the woods were even darker. Is that what she was seeing--the darkness? Surely there was some metaphor there, one that could speak to the dark times in life. Yes, the times were dark, but there would be light again.

Quinton sighed.

Maybe the best thing for Audria was to let her go. The thought felt like a stabbing pain, but seeing Audria hurt tonight was worse. Quinton tossed the idea around in his head, working to weigh the pros and cons. All the cons were selfish--he wanted to be with her. But love was patient, and kind, and not self-seeking. Audria needed space. She needed someone to be patient with her. He could do that--from a distance.

Letting her go would hurt, yes, but staying and causing her more pain simply wasn't an option. If she wanted to be with him, to move forward, it would have to be her decision, and at her own pace. Quinton swiped a hand over his face. Did he have the strength to tell her? Did he have the strength to let her go? No, but God did, and Quinton would trust God to give him the strength do what needed to be done. But when? When would he break things off? On Christmas day? No way. The day was difficult enough for her.

He pressed a fist to his mouth, knuckles pressing into his bottom lip and prayed. *God, show me what to do and when to do it. Give me the words. Give me the strength. And bring her back to me when she's ready, 'cause I'll be waiting.*

The car rolled into the cabin drive, and Mr. Rylatt turned off the engine. Audria was first out of the car, arms wrapped around her body. Mrs. Rylatt was next. She rushed toward Audria.

Mr. Rylatt tapped the steering wheel and gave a short whistle. "Here we go."

What did that mean?

Mr. Rylatt eased from the car, and then there they were--just Quinton and Maddox. They sat, both watching Audria move quickly up the cabin stairs, her parents following behind.

Maddox smacked Quinton's knee. "Have you ever seen her angry?"

"She's angry?" 'Cause he would've put money on a different emotion. "Pretty sure she's hurting."

"And angry," Maddox said. "And that's a terrifying combination."

Quinton gulped. "Does she get angry often?"

"No," he said, and paused. "It takes a lot to really upset her, but when she's had it, well...she's had it. Truly, the government could use an angry Audria to end the War on Terror."

What? Quinton gulped again. "What do we do?"

"Pray." Maddox arched both brows, forehead creasing. "C'mon, let's see if we can calm her down."

Quinton reached for the door handle. He watched Audria swing open the cabin door, and noticed how Mr. Rylatt lingered for more than a moment before entering.

"C'mon." Maddox tugged on Quinton's elbow. "I don't wanna go in alone."

Good Lord, what was waiting for them?

Quinton opened the car door and made his way to the cabin, Maddox matching his pace. They could hear it from the bottom step--Audria's rage.

"She has red hair." Maddox winced and gave Quinton a one shouldered shrug.

He nodded, and they entered.

"You knew about this, didn't you?" Audria's voice boomed. She pointed a finger at her mom and dad, face red, mascara smeared from the tears. Quinton stayed near the door. "You knew Clay's parents were here. You planned this."

Of course, Audria's family would never do something like this. Quinton kept quiet in the entryway and watched Mrs. Rylatt as she held out open palms. She shook her head. "Honey, we would never. We're so--"

"Stop it. Just stop it." Audria swiped her eyes. "Clay is dead. He's dead."

"Tooter," her Dad said, but she stopped him.

"I miss him." She visibly shook, sobs hitching in her throat. "And now his parents hate me."

They didn't hate her. The opposite, actually. Quinton closed the door and eased into the kitchen beside Maddox.

"I refuse to stay here any longer," Audria said, voice shaking. "I can't do this."

Quinton's heart writhed in his chest. *Oh, to hold her right now. To ease her pain.* Would she let him? He started forward, but Maddox stepped in front and crossed the room. He wrapped his long arms around his sister.

"It's okay. It's okay," Maddox said in a soothing tone. "We love you."

Quinton swallowed back tears.

"Let me go!" she screamed and struggled. "This all your fault. Everyone. It's your fault. If you would have left me alone, I'd be fine. I'm fine without all of you."

Quinton's heart shattered.

"Audria, stop it." Maddox held her tighter and kissed her cheek. "We've got you. It's okay."

"You've all made it worse," she screamed. "I'm even more confused because you people keep trying to push me with someone I just met."

Quinton shook his head. *She wasn't ready.* And she was right. Everyone had been trying to push them together.

Yes, it might kill him, but he had to let her go.

Chapter Nineteen

AUDRIA CURLED UP in the armchair in the corner of her cabin room. She held onto the mug of hot chocolate Mom had brought up. Mom knew when not to press and settled for a kiss on the cheek instead of a conversation. But maybe Audria needed to talk right now, if not with Mom, then with someone...

Seeing Clay's parents. The shock of it. Like reliving Clay's death all over again.

A tear raced down the side of her face and puddled in the corner of her lip. She pressed it away with a knuckle.

And poor Quinton. The look of helplessness on his face was crushing. What was she even thinking, falling for another soldier? He, too, could be gone, killed in action, like Clay. Her heart couldn't take such a risk.

She sniffed and drew her knees closer to her chest and pulled a knit blanket from the armrest. The clock ticked. Eleven forty-seven. Minutes passed. Another Christmas Eve faded away. Quinton once talked about the hope Christmas brought. Maybe for most, but it seemed Christmas brought only hurt for her.

Her phone buzzed on the armrest. A text from Nora. It read, **How did it go?**

As if Nora hadn't heard already.

A simple text. A simple question, but the answer, well, Audria wasn't even sure she knew the answer.

Texting Nora back wouldn't do, so Audria picked up the phone and called.

"Hey," Nora said.

"Sorry so late."

"No biggie. You okay?"

Yes, Nora knew. Audria let out a long sigh. "I blew it. All of it."

"How were Clay's parents?"

Audria pinched the bridge of her nose, eyes closed. "Nora, Mr. Smith looked so much like Clay, and I hadn't seen either of them in so long, and there I was..." The words poured out. "I was holding hands with Quinton, and he told me loved me, and--"

"He loves you? What did you say?"

"I didn't. Clay's parents were there, and I...I ran."

"Oh, girl, I'm so sorry."

"They didn't deserve that. And Quinton didn't either."

"How are things now?"

"Quiet. Sad." She rocked her head from side to side and set her mug on the small table close by. "I yelled at everyone when we got back to the cabin. It was terrible." Another tear fell. "Nora, I said things I don't think anyone can forgive me for."

Nora didn't reply.

"Part of me thought, or wondered for a moment..." Audria sniffled and wiped at her nose. She chewed on her thumbnail and then let her hand drop over a knee. "I wondered if my family had planned this, too. Planned for

Clay's parents to show up. Everyone has been working so hard to make sure Quinton and I met and got to know each other and went on a date...I thought maybe..."

"They would never do that. Never. I would never do that. And I'm sorry, Audria. You know I love you. I shouldn't have meddled so much, either."

"I'm just so confused right now."

"Audria, you've come so far."

Nora was right. But maybe she had come too far too fast.

"What are you going to do now?"

"Hide up here forever."

"Not an option."

Audria grumbled and pulled the blanket up under her chin.

"Do you love him? Do you love Quinton?"

"After the things I said last night--"

"Do you love him?"

"It's not that simple."

"But it is."

"What about Clay's parents? You should have seen the hurt still in their eyes. It must have killed them to see me with another man."

"Did you talk to them about it?"

"I ran."

"Then you're making a lot of assumptions right now."

"And you're sounding too much like a principal."

"I know you're upset, but let's use reason. You won't know how they felt, or what Quinton is feeling right now, if you don't talk to them."

"How can I look at them again? I acted like an idiot."

"You acted like someone who was overwhelmed and hurting. No one blames you."

Audria sighed and stretched out her legs.

"Get some sleep. Tomorrow morning, go downstairs, talk to your family and Quinton, and enjoy Christmas together."

"I don't know if it's that simple."

"Stop worrying about what you don't know, and just be open. Try."

"Nora, I'm scared. What if...what if something happens to Quinton like..."

"Girl, God's got you. He's got all your broken parts, all your fears, and worries. We all die. It's not a reason to avoid loving someone again. Yes, you're scared. Yes, your heart has been broken, but Audria, there's so much more to life than remaining in grief. So much joy waits for you. You grab it for others--grab it for yourself."

Audria wiped her eyes with the cuff of her sleeve and reached for the hot chocolate.

"Get some rest. I'll be praying for you."

Audria pressed her lips together, chin trembling. "Thank you, Nora."

"I've always got your back."

The phone went silent, and the screen darkened. Audria sipped the now lukewarm hot chocolate. Her breathing slowed, shoulders relaxed against the back of the chair. So much to consider. So much to sort through.

She turned her head and gazed out the window. Frost formed on the panes. The moon shone bright. Audria closed her eyes and whispered a prayer.

What do I do?

***

A breakfast casserole was baking in the oven. The buttery smell wafted in the air and eased the tension in the living room. Nothing mended family quarrels like a good meal. Audria sat on the corner of the couch, legs tucked with a pillow between her knees. She sipped on her coffee, hoping someone else would be the first to talk.

Dad sat on the other end of the couch, legs propped on the coffee table, Perry cuddled up under his arm. Even Perry looked upset at her. Maddox leaned against the fireplace watching the flames, and Mom piddled with the Christmas tree lights. Quinton stood in the kitchen peering out the frosted windows. All the silence. Too much silence

"I'm sorry." Audria removed the pillow and put it on her lap like a table. "I'm sorry I yelled at all of you...I--"

"We know, baby," Mom said. She crossed the room and sat beside Audria.

"Please, forgive me," Audria said. "I acted like an idiot." Just remembering the outburst caused her face to warm.

"We forgive you," Mom said and gave her a side hug. "You had cause to be angry."

Dad turned. "Tooter, we love you. And we're sorry for pushing you so hard."

Maddox smiled. "You know I've already forgiven you."

But Quinton. What was he thinking? Feeling?

And what was she feeling?

She swallowed and nodded. "Thank you, guys, for everything. For caring for me. For helping me through...it's been..." She let the words fade.

"Can we open Christmas gifts now?" Maddox squatted, reaching for the largest gift beneath the tree.

Mom shot him a look. "We haven't had breakfast yet. And we still need to take our family picture."

"Not in our pajamas, Georgie," Dad chimed in. "And not in front of that dumb tree."

Audria used their bantering time as an excuse to leave the couch. Quinton was still standing, back toward her. He held to the counter, shoulders tensed, head low.

"Quinton?"

He turned, face drawn, giving the appearance of little sleep. Then again, she'd bet no one rested well last night.

"I'm so sorry." She inched forward, one arm crossed.

"No, I'm sorry." He shook his head. "I shouldn't have told you that I love--"

"It's me. I got scared and confused and ran, and then said things I should have never--"

"How are you?" His eyes searched hers with genuine concern.

She considered the question and shifted her weight from one foot to the other. "I'm getting there."

"Where's there?" He cracked a hint of a smile.

"It's not there-there, but somewhere closer to there-there than before."

"That made absolutely no sense."

Audria laughed, the strain between them lessening. "I know."

"Time for presents," Maddox yelled in their direction.

"Guess Mom caved." Audria shrugged, and they made their way to the living room. Quinton led her for a moment, his hand against the small of her back, but then removed his touch. Yet, she wished his touch had remained. Quinton cleared his throat and took a seat as Maddox handed out gifts.

Dad went first, opening Perry's gift. He laughed at the silly looking dog sweater and chuckled harder as he wrestled it over Perry's head. Perry pouted, but Audria was positive the spoiled animal loved the attention. Dad opened Mom's present to him next. A wooden sign with their last name inscribed. Not the best craftsmanship, but kudos to her for trying. Audria hid her smile.

"It's for our cabin, dear," Mom said to Dad. He nodded his thanks and blew her a kiss.

"Open the one I made for you," Dad said to Mom.

Audria watched them, the sparkle in their eyes. No matter their bantering, her parents loved one another. Anyone could see it. Their loved served as a model to her, to Maddox, to anyone who watched them.

Mom lifted the small box and opened the package. An envelope. Audria squinted and wished very much she'd put in her contacts. What was that?

Mom gasped. "Plans for a she-shed."

"A what?" Audria scrunched her nose. Maddox laughed, and Quinton appeared as perplexed as she.

"It's a shed," Dad said. "Like a man-cave but for the ladies."

"I've been asking you to make this for years." Mom threw her arms around Dad's neck and kissed him. "Thank you, dear."

"All right, all right." Maddox extended his arms to the side, head bobbing. "That's enough. It's my turn to give a home made gift to all of you. It's been hard to create something while being deployed, so I came up with--" He waved a hand like some sort of magician. "A game. But not just any game. A family scavenger hunt."

Audria rolled her eyes. Maddox and his crazy antics. "It's too cold for that."

"Then we'll play when I get back from deployment in May," Maddox said with a firm shake of his head.

"I love it." Mom clapped her hands, and Perry barked. Dad shushed him, and the old dog frowned.

Audria stood and knelt beneath the tree. "It's my turn."

She divvied out the presents and watched, hands clasped. One by one they pulled their blankets from the wrapping.

"They are prayer blankets," she said. "Each knot is a prayer I've said specifically for you."

Quinton held his blanket close, fingers working over

each knot. His eyes met hers, and a smile crept over his face. Her heart did that thing again...pulling, tugging, but this time it wasn't in opposite directions.

"I'd like to give all of you a gift." Quinton stood.

"Quinton, honey," Mom said. "You didn't have to make any of us gifts."

"Mr. and Mrs. Rylatt, you've shown so much love to me. You're the kind of family I pray to have one day." He knelt and passed out the gifts, handing Audria a small square box. "It's my way of saying, thank you."

Mom opened her gift first, a canvas with a wooden frame. Charcoal gray dots and dashes decorated the center of the canvas. Mom's brows knit together.

"It's Morse code," said Quinton. "It says 'family.'"

"It's beautiful." Mom stood and gave Quinton a hug.

Dad pulled his gift from the package. A hammer. He turned it over and revealed the engraving. Audria stretched her neck to see. It was a Bible verse. She squinted.

Matthew 7:24-27. BUILD YOUR HOUSE ON THE ROCK.

"This is real thoughtful, Quinton. Thank you." Dad extended his hand and met Quinton's arm with a sound clasp.

"You can use that to build my she-shed," Mom said with a short giggle.

"And I got a box full of candy? That's not homemade." Maddox arched a brow, smile wide.

"It was made in a home." Quinton shrugged and everyone laughed. "I was running out of ideas, man. Sorry."

Quinton bent and picked up a medium-sized gift bag. "I also made these."

He pulled out wooden-rounds. "They're Christmas ornaments."

"Dude," Maddox leaned forward, hands hanging over his knees. "So that's why you bought the wood-burning kit. I'm impressed."

"Me, too." Audria grinned and held out her hand as Quinton passed them out. He'd drilled a hole at the top and strung a buffalo plaid ribbon through, and tied it in a bow. On hers he had engraved a single word in cursive-- hope.

"Mine has a pretty nice rendition of Perry on it," Dad said, holding his ornament for all to see. And he was right. Quinton had used the wood-burning tool to draw a pretty decent picture of Perry on it. Perry barked, and they laughed.

Mom's said "Love," and Maddox's said, "Faith."

"Quinton, thank you. How thoughtful," Mom said. He smiled glanced toward Audria.

The room quieted. Audria pulled the ribbon and eased the lid from the small box.

Oh my. Her lips parted, fingertips pressed to her lips.

A necklace. Three dainty tiers. Rose-gold. Three small beaded bars, one on each tier. It was beautiful.

"It's Morse code, too" Quinton said. He crossed the room and knelt at her side and pointed to each line with careful movements. "It says, Faith, Hope, Love."

Her fingers skimmed across the necklace. "You made this?"

The way he watched her, words failed to express how it made her feel. Safe. Sure. Certain. He nodded. "You like it?"

She nodded.

A knock rapped at the front door, and everyone paused, sharing curious expressions and shrugs.

Dad stood and answered.

Mr. and Mrs. Smith stood at the cabin door. Audria swallowed as her throat grew dry.

"Please," Dad said. "Come in. Merry Christmas."

"Merry Christmas," Mr. Smith said. "We're sorry it's so early. We were hoping to um..."

"To talk with Audria for a moment." Mrs. Smith finished her husband's sentence.

Mom and Dad turned to Audria. She gave them a smile and a nod.

"We will all just go...do something...somewhere else." Mom rounded everyone with a wave of her hand. "And you're both welcome to stay for breakfast. There will be plenty."

"Oh, no, but thank you. We really can't stay long," Mrs. Smith said as Mr. Smith patted her hand. Mom nodded.

It must be hard enough for Mr. and Mrs. Smith to be here. Staying for breakfast would only make a hard situation more difficult. Audria folded her arms, eyes meeting Quinton's for a moment. She wasn't sure what expression lingered on his face, but it made her stomach nervous.

Quinton paused before following Maddox, and Audria turned to Mr. and Mrs. Smith. They sat at the dining table, a scene so familiar and comfortable. All the memories with them. Three years dating their son, one as his fiancé.

And now, here they were, on Christmas Day. Two years after Clay passed.

A lump rose in her throat, one that wouldn't go away.

"Today is, well, it's a tough day for us," Mrs. Smith said with a quick dab at her nose. She scooted closer to Mr. Smith. "We know it's not an easy day for you, either."

Audria lowered her eyes. Looking at them hurt.

"Audria, we are so sorry about last night," Mrs. Smith said. She reached across the table and clasped Audria's hands between hers. "If we would have known how upset..." She stopped and blinked back the tears forming in her eyes.

Mr. Smith wrapped an arm around his wife. "Clara and I want you to know we love you. We always will, and it's okay if you've found someone new. Clay would want you to move on, be open to love again."

Move on. Be open. Those phrases seemed to plague and inspire her over the past month.

"We'd like you to see something, rather, have it." Mr. Smith pulled an envelope from his pocket.

Audria tilted her head, and squinted. *A letter?*

No. A photo.

Mr. Smith handed the picture to his wife. She held it with both hands, mouth pressed in a fine line.

After many moments, Mrs. Smith released a long breath. "We knew Quinton looked familiar. Here, sweetheart. Please take it."

Mrs. Smith handed over the picture, and Audria's heart pounded in her ears. Audria cradled the photo in her palms, vision blurring through fresh tears.. She couldn't keep her bottom lip from trembling.

It was Clay. The last deployment. He stood, grinning, arms draped over Maddox and...Quinton.

Surely, she had seen this photo before, never thinking twice about the man she didn't know, only seeing Maddox and Clay. The photo was calming, yet haunting, eerie even. Her past, present, maybe even future stared back, offering a choice: To remain frozen in a past that could never be her future, or embrace a new love and a new life. Illogical perhaps, but she wanted both.

Audria opened her mouth to speak, but Mrs. Smith held up a hand.

"Please, listen," she said. "We want happiness for you. We want you to find love again and know the kind of love Sam and I have for each other. The kind of love your mom and dad have."

More tears came. They fell heavy and hot and fast. "You aren't mad?"

"Heavens no, baby." Mrs. Smith smiled. "His name is Quinton, right?"

Audria nodded.

"Do you love him?" Mrs. Smith asked and leaned forward.

Audria closed her eyes, lips pressed together. She rubbed her temple and then sighed. "I do. I do love him."

"Does he love you?" Mrs. Smith asked.

Audria nodded through the tears, wiping them away with alternating wrists.

"Then go for it." Mr. Smith swatted at the table with a hearty chuckle. "Go. For. It."

Go for it?

"Come here." Mrs. Smith scooted from the table and wrapped her arms around Audria. Audria leaned into the hug.

She could move on, be open, and go for it.

Chapter Twenty

"QUINTON." AUDRIA YELLED his name and darted up the stairs. No answer. Where was he? She checked his cabin room, knocked on the bathroom door, even ran to the basement.

Mom sat cuddled beside Dad, tissue crumbled in her hand. He held her close. Audria twisted her mouth in a pinch.

"I'm okay, guys," Audria said. "Really, I'm...I'm better than okay." Was her face glowing? It sure felt like it.

Mom sniffled and smiled.

"Where's Quinton?" Audria tucked her hair behind her ears and chewed on her bottom lip.

Mom gave Dad's knee a quick pat. "He said he was going to get some fresh air."

Maddox quirked his brows, lifted his face from a fishing magazine in the corner chair. "Check the balcony."

"Balcony, right." Audria dashed back upstairs, lungs begging for mercy. Athletics were Quinton's thing, not hers. She hurried across the landing and stood at the glass doors. There he was, coat bundled and tight across his broad shoulders, staring out over the mountains. She opened the door, and he looked over his shoulder.

"Audria? You okay?"

Her chest rose and fell faster than her thoughts. "Quinton."

He closed the gap between then. "You hurt?"

"Quinton, I love you." The words sprang forth like all new life must.

In an instant he cleared the space between them. His large hands lifted to cradle her face. Warmth spread from the top of her head to the tips of her toes.

"I love you," she said again in a whisper.

His voice hitched in his throat, and he laughed. "You love me. You love me?"

She nodded.

"You sure?"

She nodded and kissed his thumb as it skimmed over her lips.

"You're sure? 'Cause I'll wait. I'll wait for you until you're ready. I've already prayed and if I have to let you go--"

"No!" *No. No.* "Don't let me go," she said, hands clenched around his wrists. "I love--"

His lips covered hers in a crashing sensation. A familiar soft chill touched her cheeks, and flurries landed on her lashes. Her eyes fluttered open. Snow. It was snowing. Again.

Quinton pressed his forehead to hers, still cradling her face. "I guess kissing in the snow is our thing."

"I'm okay with that." She pulled his face lower and kissed him again.

Here she was moving on, being open, and going for it.

***

Audria fiddled with her knit scarf, tucking it into her red coat. She posed beside Quinton, his arm around her waist. Maddox stood next to Quinton, and Mom was next to Maddox.

"Hurry up, Dad." Maddox rubbed at his arms. "If you haven't noticed, it's snowing and freezing."

"Your mom has to have a family Christmas picture. Blame her," Dad yelled across the yard and kicked at the tripod, his version of adjusting the camera.

Audria laughed. By far, this was the best Christmas ever. So full of...of... Audria tilted her head. It was full of life, hope, faith, and love. She touched the handmade necklace hanging against her chest beneath her scarf and gave a prayer of thanks.

"Quinton," Mom said. "I love your idea for the picture. Everyone gets what they want."

"Not everyone," Maddox said through a frown and folded his arms.

Audria ignored Maddox and gave Quinton a playful nudge. "The idea was genius."

Mom wanted a Christmas tree family picture, Dad didn't want the photo but most liked the idea of the cabin making an appearance, so Quinton solved the problem. He decorated the pine tree beside the cabin with red bows. A win-win.

"It couldn't be any more perfect." Mom clasped her hands, voice at a high pitch. And she was right. The snow, the cabin, the trees, the red ribbons.

"Dad. Come on," Maddox called out again.

Dad made a final kick at the tripod, jiggled the camera a bit, and then ran toward them. They laughed, watching him tread through the snow like some sort of move from a country western dance.

"Be ready to smile," he said, sucking in deep breaths.

The red light blinked, one, two, three times.

Mom giggled. "Say, 'Merry Christmas.'"
"Merry Christmas."
They held their smiles, and the camera flashed, capturing the merriest of Christmases.

THE END

EPILOGUE

NEARLY ONE YEAR LATER

It's hard to drive with shoeboxes blocking the rear-view mirror, of course, but by now Audria was pretty much a pro. The light ahead turned yellow, and she pumped her brakes on the slick road, stopping right in time to catch it turning red. She wasn't quite positive, but near certain the road conditions were exactly like this last year at Christmastime. No wait; that might have been Black Friday. Yes, definitely Black Friday.

The light turned green, and Audria pressed the gas a bit too hard. She swatted back at the avalanche of boxes spilling into the front seat, but to no avail.

Now that she thought about it more, all of this seemed a little like déjà vu. The boxes, the weather, the boxes falling all over the place. Except the policeman. Audria laughed, recalling that particular event. Thankfully, she hadn't been pulled over in... hmmm, she tapped on her bottom lip. A year. It had been a year. Nice. Maybe her insurance would go down.

A car honked from behind. Audria rolled down the window and stuck her head out.

Blue lights. Oh no.

Seriously, Lord?

Her stomach dropped.

Audria pulled over to the side of the road. She slid down in her seat for a moment and then reached for her license and registration.

Please don't be the same officer as last year. Please. Please.

Audria squeezed her eyes shut, repeating the prayer, and felt around the front seat for her purse.

"ID and insurance."

"Here, sir." Same man. Her stomach sank lower. She

couldn't even look him in the eyes.

"Hey. It's you." He chuckled. "Long time no see."

Audria focused on the odometer of her little Accord and considered buying a new one soon. Anything to take her mind off a ticket that was sure to come her way.

"So, Ms. Rylatt, weren't you the one who got to be Randall the Rudolph Red-Nosed Raideer Reindeer in the Christmas parade?"

"That's me. Second year in a row."

"What an honor."

"Oh, it is." She shook her head. Nothing said Merry Christmas like being seen in that insane costume. And with Maddox here to experience it all--a new level of mortifying.

"Do you know why I pulled you over?"

And there she was, feeling very much like an elementary school student once again. "I really don't know, officer."

"Looks like you're still collecting empty boxes."

"They're not empty this time."

"That's what I hear."

"Sir?"

"You're the one that's been helping folks in the community, right? Putting together that Resource Rotation."

"Yes, sir. That's where I'm headed tonight. Please, sir, I don't want to be late."

He smiled. "I pulled you over to help you out."

"Help me out?"

"The police force would like to come and serve tonight. Work with the community in a positive light."

"That's wonderful."

"And I've been asked to give you a personal escort to the event."

Audria grimaced. "Um, okay. By who?"

"That's confidential ma'am."

Weird. "Okay...can we get going then?"

He nodded and waddled away. She watched him get into his car and drive ahead then wave for her to follow.

Kind of cool.

She reached for her cell and called Nora. No answer. And no missed calls either.

She called Quinton. No answer.

Neither Mom nor Maddox answered.

A thin line of sweat began to form on her brow. Hopefully everyone was in their place already and setting up. Families would be at the doors in an hour, and there was still so much to do. This was the first night of the Resource Rotation. The first night couldn't flop. She'd worked so hard to extend the event dates from one night to three, in order to accommodate more families.

She worked to push her worry aside and drew in deep breaths.

They arrived at the church, and Audria was relieved to see Nora's car in the parking lot. Maddox was here. Mom, Dad, and Quinton. *Whew.*

The officer opened her door and said, "Don't worry about the boxes, ma'am. I'll have my men bring them in."

She nodded, thankful, but still perplexed. What was happening? Audria stepped onto the sidewalk and opened the church doors. What a beautiful sight. A winter wonderland.

Oh, Nora had outdone herself with the decor. White shimmering Christmas trees everywhere. Icicle lights hung from the ceiling.

The families were going to flip when they saw this. Audria passed by the resource tables, hands skimming across the white linen table cloths. The lights above grew dim. Where was everyone? In the kitchen?

She peeked around the corner. No one.

Soft instrumental music began to play. Audria turned to see Quinton walking toward her, dressed in...a suit?

"Quinton?" Audria smoothed a hand down the side of her black dress and clutched her purse.

He smiled as he drew closer and wrapped an arm around her waist greeting her with a kiss.

"You look beautiful," he said.

"What's going on? Where is everyone?"

"They'll be here in a second, but I wanted a moment alone with you."

"Quinton, I have a ton of boxes that are about to--"

"Just a minute," he said and kissed her once more. He intertwined their fingers, and she met his gaze. Those eyes. That smile.

Thank you, God, for bringing him home safe. Here he was, this Godly man who stood before her, no knelt before her. Wait. Knelt? Audria swallowed. Her hand flew to her chest.

"Quinton?"

He looked up at her, on bended knee, holding a little black box with a ring. A diamond ring. Her heart pounded inside her head.

"Audria Rylatt, I love you. I love your heart for God, and I love your heart for others. If you'll have me, I'll strive to be the man you deserve, the man God wants for you. Will you marry me?"

"Yes!" She knelt in front of him on both knees, smiling through her tears, and kissed him. He slid the diamond on her ring finger, and it glistened in the glow of the lights.

A flood of cheers filled the room. Family and friends gathered close. Hugs, kisses, high fives. Audria turned at a gentle touch.

Mr. and Mrs. Smith. They came. Audria pressed her hands over her mouth. They cried and embraced.

Here they were, all moving on, being open, and going for it.

FUN FACTS ABOUT
"CHRISTMAS ON A MISSION"

1: Audria's nickname was Tooter. Poor girl. I have a few parent-given nicknames: Tinker, Hannah-bell, and Hannie, but my dad did call me Tootles when I was younger. Not sure why he called me that. Hoping it's not for the same reason Audria was called Tooter.

2: My family and I rented a cabin in Gatlinburg not too long ago. The layout in the book was the same layout of the cabin where we stayed. We also had a raccoon visitor each night that we lovingly named Rocky. One night, we couldn't even get outside to go to the hot tub because he was guarding the door. Crazy little beast.

3: I had never once made macarons in my life until this book. They are delicious, but making them is quite the process. Audria has mad macaron making skills...I do not.

4: Audria got pulled over a few times. I've been pulled over a time or two or three. Okay, maybe four or more. Speeding yes, but one time it was for popping a U-turn. I tried to explain to the officer that there wasn't a sign saying I couldn't do a U-turn, but I still got a ticket.

5: Quinton worked at a toy store when he was in high school, and so did I! I was hired as a seasonal worker, but they kept me on past Christmas. I stayed with them for two years, but never insulted a customer like Quinton did.

6: Our church totally hosts an event similar to the Resource Rotation Audria puts together in this story. We work through the school system to identify families in need and then allow them to come, shop, connect, and speak with a pastor and/or counselor. It's beautiful. I would encourage your school, church, business, or group to host your own "Resource Rotation."

7: The story takes place in Clarksville, Tennessee, a real place not far from Nashville. My family and I live in Clarksville and love it! However, Richland Middle is a made-up school, as is the Raideer mascot--too bad.

8: Like Audria and Nora, I am a big fan of Mexican food

and trivia nights, but unlike them, I've never won one, nor have I received a medal for my attempts. I don't even think they give medals to the trivia night winners in real life, but they totally should.

9: Audria's family has an RV, and I secretly want one. #Jealous.

10: Perry the Pug was inspired by this older little pug who occasionally roams our neighborhood. While I like pugs, we have a beautiful white lab mix named Albus Dumbledore Conway (Yes, he's named after the greatest wizard Hogwarts has ever seen).

Georgie's Famous Leftover Thanksgiving Turkey Soup
Recipe by Brenda Conway (aka My Hubby's Aunt)

It's simple and no real measurements. Simply follow the steps to a delicious bowl of Leftover Thanksgiving Turkey Soup.
1: Place turkey bones in a large pot.
2: Cover with water and add a heaping spoonful of all the leftovers you have. This may include potatoes, dressing, sweet potatoes, glazed carrots, squash, green beans,
corn, cranberry sauce, gravy etc.
3: Boil about 2 hours
4: Strain, and now you have your turkey broth to use as a soup, or to add to any dish of your choosing.
5: Salt and pepper to taste.
6: Feel free to leave in the corn, carrots, and green beans or add other vegetables like celery or chopped potatoes. This dish pairs well with crackers, a sandwich, side
salad or on its own.
7: Enjoy!

Hot-Chocolate For the Holidays
Recipe by Karen Hines (aka My Mom)

1/2 cup of sugar
1/2 cup of cocoa powder of your choice
4 1/3 cup of whole milk
1 tsp of vanilla extract

1: Mix sugar and cocoa in pan.
2: Stir in small amount of measured out milk (about 1/4 to 1/3 cup).
3: Cook over medium heat.
4: Bring to a boil and stir for approximately two minutes.
5: Stir in the rest of the milk and vanilla.
6: Just heat to how warm you like it.
7: Enjoy!

AUTHOR NOTE

Dear Reader,

First off, thank you for picking up this book and giving it a go! It's an honor to know you chose a book of mine out of all the books out there. Thank you.

If you've enjoyed this story, I would absolutely love if you'd be willing to leave a quick review on Amazon and/or Goodreads. Nothing big, a word or two--maybe a sentence or two if you're feeling generous. Letting others know about a good book you've read is the BEST way to show the author some serious love, so I want to thank you in advance for the love.

Okay, so I'm hoping you enjoyed Audria and Quinton's story as much as I have. I also hope you enjoyed Audria's family, too! And, Nora--isn't she the best? I'm seriously sad they are fictitious characters!

This story has lived in my head for over two years. It started with an idea about a care package reaching a soldier and then took shape from there. The first scene I wrote was actually the scene where Audria and Quinton are in Gatlinburg standing on the bridge about to kiss, but that was all I had. Truly, Gatlinburg is one of our family's favorite places to visit. It is indeed romantic, and I wanted to capture a bit of that romance in this particular scene. It wasn't until later in the writing process that I decided Audria needed to face a little of her past. Sometimes we all need to face our past so we can move on.

I've learned that moving on from our past successfully often means we help others along the way, so it only made sense to me that Audria needed to have a heart for others. I knew she worked with students, but wasn't sure in what capacity. During a staff meeting at school (I teach 7th graders), I learned that our school system had a Homeless Liaison, and it clicked--Audria had to be a Homeless Liaison. I'm honestly not sure what that staff meeting was all about, because I was researching the job description, which looks similar to the things Audria does in the story.

When I got home, the story simply came to me. Typically, writing doesn't come that easy for me, but this story came, and it has inspired me to *be open, and go for it* in whatever God has called me to do. I pray 'Christmas on a Mission" inspires the same in you.

If you're reading this around Christmastime, MERRY CHRISTMAS from me to you! Cuddle up with some hot chocolate, maybe a macaron or two or three, and enjoy.

Again, THANK YOU for choosing this book! Sending love and hugs your way!

Love,

Hannah R. Conway

Stay up to date with my quarterly newsletter! Sign up at http://bit.ly/HannahsNewsletter

AUTHOR BIO

Hannah Conway is a military wife, mother of two, middle school teacher, best-selling author, and speaker. Her novels are a deployment experience of their own, threaded with faith, and filled with twists and turns.Hannah is a member of the American Christian Fiction Writers, and My book Therapy. She and her family live in Tennessee.

Visit Hannah at hannahrconway.com

OTHER BOOKS BY HANNAH

WEDDING A WARRIOR
Her faith is stretched, and her once planned path is blurred. There's much to consider, and saying yes to either man would change the trajectory of her life. Which path should she take?

THE WOUNDED WARRIOR'S WIFE
Are some wounds too deep, and some marriages too broken, that they fall beyond even God's ability to restore?

UP IN SMOKE
Sparks begin to fly and their love is rekindled, a marriage of convenience will either make their wildest dreams come true or cause their best-laid plans to go up in smoke.

UP IN SMOKE

CHAPTER ONE

Leanna Wilson couldn't seem to shake the chill from her bones, and it wasn't because of a lack of warm bodies filling up the funeral home parlor. She cupped her hands around her nose and mouth and breathed in and out, in and out, warding off the next panic attack.

The hills of Kentucky called her home, but not in the way she expected. Why hadn't she returned like promised? Before this?

She longed for the warmth of her parents' kitchen. The savory smells of comfort wafting about the air. Vegetable soup. Fresh bread.

Echoes of their laughter danced throughout her memories.

Laughing. Mom and Dad always laughed. Leanna attempted a smile. Unable to stand any longer to greet the mourners, she sat in the front row on-looking the twin caskets, supported by a rickety wooden white chair. Its cushion, well worn, matched the color of her sister's tear-stained cheeks.

No nine-year-old child should lose so much. Leanna consoled her sister, one arm holding her close, though her attempts were as foreign as her relationship with Brie. A seventeen-year age difference did nothing to decrease the gap.

Brie was still pasting Band-Aids on her body as stickers by the time Leanna graduated college. Back then they were close. Visits during summer breaks and holidays included piggy-back rides, finger painting, and braiding Barbie doll hair.

Leanna tucked her chin, face warming with the memories bittersweet. Yes, she and Brie had been close, but back then, Leanna considered herself close to all her friends and family. Much had changed. Too much.

Brie neither stirred nor stiffened when Leanna squeezed her small hand, but sat, slumped forward. Her soft honey curls veiled her face but couldn't hide the sobs, or the tears that dripped from her cheek.

The cries twisted Leanna's heart, the burning sensation almost too much to bear. She clamped her bottom lip between her teeth, eyes closed. Why hadn't she returned sooner?

No reason came to mind, only pitiful excuses.

Lamenting sobs, like nails driving into the layers of grief and regret in her soul, echoed around the room. How many more hours did they have to endure this? And tomorrow, the funeral.

Another hand touched her shoulder. Another. Then another. So many people, compassionate people, offering condolences. Their words she could not hear. Their faces, familiar, but indistinguishable. Her hand trembled at her side against the black burdet dress--a gift to herself from a trendy boutique during her travels in Europe.

Europe. Leanna rolled her neck, breathing in the memories of that summer, but the cobble stone roads, rainy days, and ancient castles of Europe couldn't hold her focus. Tattered carpet, thick air saturated with a floral scent, and twin caskets took precedence in her mind.

Leanna held to the soft coal-colored fabric of the dress meant to be worn at cocktail parties and other social elite events in New York, never at her parents' funeral. Her throat constricted. She swallowed, but the tightness remained, and the chill returned. Leanna shook, and the diamond on her left ring finger hung loose. It caught on the threads of the cushion. She tugged it free and moved the engagement ring into place, but the stone sent a series of shivers through her body.

Marrying William had also been in the plan, but not anymore. He could keep his daddy's money and expensive apologies.

Why had she not taken the ring off yet? A year a part, six months since the breakup. It was she that ended the relationship, but the ring still sat in place, like a bad omen, or something chaining her to him--a man she'd tried to rid herself from for over a year now. This time it was for good, permanent, like death. This time she'd hold her ground and refuse to return to him.

Leanna slid the rock from her finger, glanced at it once, and then let it fall to the bottom of her purse. It was time to start fresh--start over. But here? Back home in Lebanon Junction, Kentucky?

Mom and Dad were gone. They'd left her to mourn-- and Brie too.

And now, Leanna was alone, helpless, and...

Hopeless.

The word scrolled through her mind. As she surveyed the room and the child at her side, hopeless fit.

Why weren't her parents alive? Alive so she could apologize, hug their necks, and bury her head on their shoulders.

Leanna blinked, and a fresh tear raced down her cheek. She swiped it away. No crying. Not now. Her stomach turned, and her chest grew heavy, threatening to crush her. She couldn't raise her eyes to meet those of the funeral guests any longer, and instead focused on her parents lying there, lifeless, still.

They could be sleeping. If only that were true.

If she could only wake them. They'd welcome her into their arms, laugh, and beg to hear all about New York. They'd help her figure out her path in life, which until now seemed so clear--something both comforting and terrifying.

It was clear she'd graduate law school, and she did. She'd been lucky to secure a paid internship at a firm in New York, and now with close to a year of experience under her belt, the firm offered her a solid position. A position full of promise, and more money than she'd seen this side of the Appalachians. She readily accepted a month ago, but now?

Life seemed so uncertain. Leanna held in a breath, and pulled Brie closer.

She rubbed her hand up and down the length of Brie's arm. The motion steadied her perhaps more than it consoled Brie. A low familiar tune deep within her memory worked its way forward. Leanna let the low melody slip from her mouth in a hum--a hymn her mother once sang. Brie stiffened but soon melted against Leanna. She swung her arm around Leanna's waist and held tight.

Leanna pressed her lip into a fine line, and tucked her chin. She never should have left for New York. Kentucky had plenty of great universities, but unlike the dullness of the funeral home and the rust-covered buildings of her hometown, New York sparkled and called. It promised a better life, more money, and happiness. Was it her, or New York, who had lied?

"Shhh, Brie. We're okay." Leanna kissed the top of Brie's wavy blond hair and hoped her words were true. "We're going to be fine." She pressed her cheek atop Brie's head and breathed her in. Brie smelled like home. Honeysuckle, soap, something baking in the oven.

Leanna closed her eyes. Her heart ached.

Brie whimpered. Leanna winced at the heart-piercing sound, and steadied her breathing.

She pushed Brie's hair back, and pulled her closer. "We'll get through this."

Brie lifted her head. Her eyes, once curious by nature,

held only uncertainty. How much she had grown. Her rounded cheeks had begun to lengthen. She no longer wore Band-Aids as stickers, or swung her legs to the beat of a tune in her head. Did she still demand sprinkles on her toast, or read Christmas stories all year long?

A lump rose in Leanna's throat. Yes, they were sisters, but right now they were strangers. It had taken the death of their parents for this realization.

The weight of Brie's stare forced Leanna further into the chair. The child staring back needed so much. Much more than what Leanna could offer.

"I love you, Brie. And...and I'm going to do my best to take care of you."

Brie tucked her lip under her top teeth, eyes shifting to her hand. She hadn't uttered a word since the car accident, and bore the gash across her forehead in silence. The doctors said she was still in shock, and rightfully so. It could be days until Brie found her voice, but even in her silence, she said so much.

Well-wishers held tissues to their noses and dabbed at their eyes as they passed in front of the caskets. They stopped patting both Leanna and Brie on the back with pursed-lips too full of sorrow.

The funeral home director, arranged the flowers at the front of the room. More arrived. The sweet floral scents repulsed her. She swallowed back the bile.

As a child, she and Dad stopped along the roadsides to pick flowers, relishing their fragrance. They brought them home to Mom, who delighted in making them the centerpiece at the dinner table. A Mason jar and wildflowers.

Leanna buried her teeth into her bottom lip.

There weren't any flowers on her parents' table today-- only on their coffins. She held her breath and shut her eyes, embracing the burning sensation growing in her lungs. Her lashes fluttered open as she sucked in a gulp of air.

She scanned the room through blurred vision. Fragrant blooming bouquets lined the side walls and filled the front and back of the ever-shrinking room. But one bouquet gave her pause.

A bright bundle with buds beginning to droop, stuffed in the corner, made her stomach pinch. Scrawled handwriting, too familiar for comfort, poked from behind a red bloom.

William.

No sight of him, but the flowers? Those were from him, for sure. He'd sent the same arrangement to her door countless times. Well wishes, but mostly apologies she'd stupidly forgiven, and now, he sent condolences.

Her heart was too numb to care.

Leanna puffed her cheeks and wiped at her forehead.

She scanned the room once more. No sign of him. Maybe he finally took the hint and moved on. Then again, the flowers suggested not.

Perhaps starting over here would prove more difficult than she hoped. Leanna cradled Brie close and kissed her wavy hair. Where else was there to go? Taking Brie to New York and away from the only home she'd ever known wasn't an option. Right now at least.

God help me.

Would that count as a prayer? It had to. But was God still listening?

Leanna rocked side to side and fought to keep her hum steady, but failed.

Grab your copy of UP IN SMOKE now!

Made in the USA
Middletown, DE
04 March 2019